My *East Coast* KILLA

Grei & Knight

A NOVEL BY

MISHA

DEDICATION

This book, I would like to dedicate to myself. I can't believe that this is book #15!
It's not easy, but it's my passion, and I wouldn't change it for the world!

Royalty Publishing House is now accepting manuscripts from aspiring or experienced urban romance authors!

WHAT MAY PLACE YOU ABOVE THE REST:

Heroes who are the ultimate book bae: strong-willed, maybe a little rough around the edges but willing to risk it all for the woman he loves.

Heroines who are the ultimate match: the girl next door type, not perfect - has her faults but is still a decent person. One who is willing to risk it all for the man she loves.

The rest is up to you! Just be creative, think out of the box, keep it sexy and intriguing!

If you'd like to join the Royal family, send us the first 15K words (60 pages) of your completed manuscript to submissions@royaltypublishinghouse.com

Check Out the LiT Reader App!

The LiT Reader App is a unique digital space with a diverse number of genres, written by both indie and formally published authors.

Download the LiT Reader App now to read FREE BOOKS! Check it in the App Store or on Google Play!

GREI OKOYE

Standing in the mirror, I smoothed my hands down the fire red dress that I was wearing. The dress clung to every curve on my body, putting my wide hips and slim waist on full display. On my feet were a pair of black red bottoms, and in my ears were a pair of diamond earrings that Tommy bought me over a year ago for Christmas, with the matching tennis bracelet that was on my wrist.

My twenty-six-inch bundles were bone straight with a part down the middle, showing off my perfectly beat face. Tommy had paid for me to pamper myself for the day, getting my hair, nails, feet, and makeup done. It was a part of his sorry package. Every time he did something, he found a way to pamper me in place of saying sorry or to stop doing the bullshit that he continued to do.

"Damn, you look good." Tommy whispered in my ear and kissed me on my right cheek as he wrapped his arms around my waist.

I looked in the mirror at him with eyes that were fed up and cold. Tommy was wearing a dark gray long sleeve button-up with a pair of light blue denim jeans that fit him perfectly, and on his feet were a pair of Clarks that was the same color of his shirt. He looked nice, as he always did, because he was a man that took pride in himself. That was what attracted me to him the most.

"Thanks."

This was how it always went. He would fuck me over, make up for it, then think that everything was okay. Little did he know, I stopped forgiving him a long time ago.

"You ready? The party started over an hour ago." He backed up from me and looked at the black and gold Rolex watch on his wrist and started walking out of the room.

"Yeah." I sighed as I followed behind him.

The last thing I wanted to do was go to a club full of people and be social. I didn't even want to be around Tommy's ass. All I wanted was to chill at home, and he could go out by himself, but of course, he wanted me to be his arm candy; his trophy wife.

"I can't wait to get you back here and fuck that fucking attitude up out of you," Tommy said through gritted teeth before opening the door for me.

Whap!

He slapped my ass as I walked in front of him. I didn't say anything; there was no emotion from me whatsoever. It had been so rare lately for him to even get a reaction out of me. I really wondered if he even noticed that his actions didn't move me anymore, because I was so fucking fed up.

Walking to the passenger door of his black 2018 Rolls Royce, I waited as Tommy locked up the house and came to open the door for me. Sliding onto the leather seats, I waited as he closed the door, and I proceeded to put my seat belt on. Tommy got into the driver's seat and started the car. The AC that was already on instantly started to blow in my face.

It was the end of June and hot as hell, even though the sun was no longer out. The night heat would still sweat out the straightest hair and the most slicked down edges. Tommy pulled out of our driveway while blasting DMX, and I looked out the window, not facing him once. He put his hand on my thigh, and I rolled my eyes up into my head.

Things weren't always like this. I used to love the shit out of Tommy Banks. He used to touch me, and I would feel all types of shocks through my body. His touch used to make me cream in my panties from the softness of his hands. Now, I cringed when he touched me and counted the seconds until his hands were removed from my body, like now.

Tommy was handsome, always had been, and probably always would be. He was six feet two and light skinned with a head full of short curls. He always made it a thing to tell people that he was Dominican, like someone actually gave a fuck. Like being Dominican was the only way that you could have curly hair, which wasn't true at all. Tommy was conceited, and I mean he did have a reason to be, but that same confidence I was attracted to had made him too cocky.

He was the biggest kingpin here in Rochester, New York, and people of all races respected the hell out of him. Tommy was rich beyond belief, and he made sure that people knew. He was the flashy type that always had to have the latest cars and the most expensive clothing and jewelry. It was all cool in the beginning, but he was now thirty and I was twenty-four. To me, there were things more important than what I was wearing and what I drove, like my sanity.

Four years ago, when I met him, he sweet talked the fuck out of me, and I ate it all up. For the first two years, I was silly putty in this nigga's hands. Tommy was slick, but now I could see through all of the bullshit. Grei Okoye was no longer a fool for Tommy Banks, and it wouldn't be long before he realized it.

Twenty minutes later, we pulled up to Club Truffle, and I could tell how packed it was inside just from the outside. The line was wrapped around the block. Tommy pulled up right in front, and as soon as he did, all eyes were on us. His license plate read 'Tommy1', so people already knew just exactly who it was.

Tommy pulled the rearview mirror down and started to check himself out. He made sure his curls were in place and sucked in his pink bottom lip. I remember when I used to love sucking on that bottom lip; just the taste of it used to make me wet. Finally, he finished giving himself the once over and closed the rearview mirror.

"You ready?" he asked as he looked over at me.

"Are *you* ready is the real question," I replied as I shook my head from side to side and took my seat belt off.

"What? What the fuck does that mean, Grei?" he asked me with his face scrunched up.

"Nothing." I breathed deeply, trying to avoid the argument that was about to happen. "Are you ready?" I asked, looking at him in the driver's seat.

His face was turning red, and I could almost see smoke coming from his ears. He looked like his head was about to explode from his body at any moment.

"Look, I'm trying to be civil with ya black ass, but if you keep on with this stank ass attitude, then I'mma whoop ya ass. You think last week was something, but that wasn't nothing. You'll wish you were fucking dead."

My eyes became wide as I watched his chest heave up and down. He was pissed just from a small comment. It seemed like everything I said ticked him off, and that was why I kept giving him short answers.

"Now, get out the car, and just shut the fuck up for the rest of the night. All I need you to do is sit by my side and look like the bad bitch that you are. Nothing more, nothing less."

"Okay." I nodded my head up and down.

I was still recovering from the ass whooping that he mentioned from last week, so it was in my best bet to just shut the fuck up for once. Tommy got out of the car and walked around my side to let me out. People in lines were still staring as I put on my bitch face. The face that told the onlookers that I loved my life, and it was a life that they wished they had. Oh, how that was a damn lie though.

Tommy held my hand as we walked into the club and through a sea of people. He slapped up people on the way and even kissed some women on the cheek in front of me. I wouldn't be surprised if he was fucking some of these bitches. I had never caught him red-handed, but I had a feeling that he was out here fucking anything moving.

Finally, we reached the VIP section, which was blocked off with a royal blue velvet rope. As soon as the bouncers saw Tommy, they opened it up without glimpsing at the clipboard that held the guest list, I'm assuming. VIP was packed, but there was a bit more room as we made our way through and over to where the man of the hour was.

"What's up, bruh?" Tommy reached out his hand and slapped up a man I knew as Knight.

"What's up, man?" he replied as he slapped him up and nodded his head at me.

His eyes scanned me from head to toe, making me feel as if I was wearing a see-through dress. He licked his lips and his eyes matched mine. The heartbeat between my thighs began to thump, matching the fast heartbeat that was in my chest.

"Come sit down." Tommy pulled me out of my trance as he yanked on my arm and guided me to a seat that was adjacent to Knight.

I didn't know why, but my insides were smiling at the thought of being able to look at his fine ass all night. Opposite of Tommy, Knight was dark skinned, about six feet four, with a set of pearly white teeth. He was wearing all black and looking good as hell in it. I was a sucker for a man in all black. Knight was wearing a pair of black jeans that were skinny but not tight like some of these dudes wore.

His shirt was black with two red and green stripes down the side, and it said Gucci in red and green in the center of the shirt. On his feet were a pair of black and gold Jordans, and his belt was black with a gold Gucci logo in front. The gold in the shoes could have thrown the outfit off, but it actually accentuated it.

Sitting down next to Tommy, I put my black clutch bag in my lap.

"Here. Have a drink," he said as he handed me a glass of champagne.

Taking the glass from his hands, I took a sip from it as I scanned the crowd. The club was packed, and there were decorations every-where, not just VIP. Everything was black, gold, and white, but it was mostly black and gold. There was a banner that read 'Happy Birthday, Knight.' I took another glimpse at him as I sipped from the cham-pagne flute.

He was holding a gold bottle of Belaire up to his sexy ass lips. Knight was also a major player in these streets and was well respected

5

by everyone. Tonight, the club was packed with people here to cele-
brate his birthday. The men wanted to work for him, and the bitches
wanted a chance to be with him. I wasn't a woman that was always in
the streets, but even I knew this much.

From what I knew, Knight worked for Tommy, and that was one
of the reasons why we were here. They were somewhat like associates
but more like business partners. As I watched him intently, I cringed
when I saw a woman walk up to him, and he looked her up and down
the same way he had looked at me. She was a beautiful woman, and
she had a huge smile on her face, showing that she liked the little
attention that he was giving her.

Rolling my eyes up in my head, I turned my attention elsewhere as
I continued to look around the crowd of people. Almost immediately,
I spotted someone that I knew. It was my cousin Farah that I hadn't
talked to in years. We had been close since we were little girls, but my
family didn't approve of my relationship with Tommy, and he basically made me cut ties with them.

She was one of the people that supported me, even though she
didn't care for him, and I still ended up ending our close relationship.
I regretted that shit so much. I was now wishing that I hadn't been so
stupid and had cut ties with him instead.

"I'm going to the bathroom," I leaned over and whispered into
Tommy's ear.

He had a cigar in his mouth and just nodded his head, halfway
acknowledging me as I followed his eyes, and he was watching a
woman that was sitting across from us. She was dressed in a black
latex halter dress that was skin tight. She could barely cross her legs,
but that didn't stop her from doing it. Shaking my head, I downed my
glass of champagne then set it on the table that was in front of us and
grabbed my clutch before getting up and walking away.

As I walked toward the bar, I was hoping that my cousin was still
there. I couldn't see through the sea of people, so all I could do was
hope that she didn't walk away before I got there. It took me a couple
of minutes to get to the bar, but when I did, I spotted her sitting down
at the bar, sipping on a drink. Farah looked as pretty as she always

had. She was dressed in a black latex skirt that had a split in the front with a matching crop top.

I wasn't at all surprised to see her showing stomach, even though we were raised to be fully clothed. We were raised Muslim and were raised to never show so much skin. I mean, in elementary school, we were able to wear short sleeve shirts and shorts, but our shorts had to be beneath our knees. Nothing was ever to be too revealing. My cousin Farah was the wild card. She never listened to anything, while I was the good one that had ended up shunned by the family.

"Hi, Farah," I greeted her.

She didn't see me walk up on her because she was looking in her phone, but when she turned and locked eyes with me, surprisingly, a smile spread across her face.

"Grei! Oh my God! Hi!" Standing up, she reached out, and we both embraced each other.

It felt great to see her and to get a hug from her because it seemed like I needed it the most right now.

"What are you doing here? I've never known you to go out to the club."

Sighing, she responded, "Well, a lot has changed since we last spoke."

Farah sat back down at the bar, and I sat on the stool next to her. Her long black hair that she usually sported was now cut into a blonde blunt cut bob. It looked amazing against her brown skin tone.

"I'm so sorry I haven't talked to you." I shook my head as I spoke. "It's just, none of the family liked Tommy, and what was I supposed to do? I was in love with him, ya know?"

"Was?" she asked.

Farah was one of those people that could always see through whatever, and I should have known that she would catch on to me talking about the love I had for him in past tense. Before I could even answer her, a voice interrupted.

"I thought you were going to the bathroom." Tommy slithered like a snake in my ear.

My flesh began to crawl as he wrapped his arms around me and

7

rubbed on my shoulder. Just the small gesture made me throw up inside of my mouth.

"Hello, Farah," Tommy greeted her as if they were friends.

He wasn't dumb. He knew that my family couldn't stand his ass, and he couldn't stand them either. Before, Tommy would try to put on a fake face and front for them, but then I think he got tired of that, so he pulled me away from them.

"Hi," Farah responded dryly and took a sip from the glass that was in front of her.

"Tommy, I was on my way to the bathroom, and I saw Farah. I just wanted to say hi, and then I was going to use the bathroom and make my way to VIP."

Bending down to my ear, he whispered through gritted teeth, "Don't fucking play with me, Grei. Go use the bathroom, and get your black ass back to the fucking section."

Trying to keep my composure, I looked back at him and smiled while he flashed me a fake ass smile as well. Tommy would never show his true colors. He would always wait until we were behind closed doors to show the real demon that he was. Without another word, he turned around and started back toward the section.

"He's still his controlling self, huh?" Farah commented.

"You don't even know the half. Can I have your number so that we can keep in touch? I know it's been a while, but I really miss the hell out of you. I don't care if Tommy doesn't approve of our relationship; I rather he be mad than us not talk," I spoke truthfully.

"Of course, babe. Fuck his old ass." She laughed.

After taking her number, we hugged, and I headed to the bathroom. The whole time that I walked, I could feel a pair of eyes watching me that I knew belonged to none other than Tommy. He was pissed, and when we got home, only the Lord knew what I was in store for.

KNIGHT YOUNG

"*D*amn, you so fucking sexy," Simone purred into my ear, sounding just like a cat.

We were on the elevator headed to the floor of my condo, and she wasn't letting up. I already knew what she wanted, but her ass wasn't even trying to wait until we got to my crib. She was standing in front of me, facing me, with her hands in my pants, massaging all ten inches of my dick. I knew she was already wet and wasn't wearing any panties, because I had slipped my hand under her hot pink dress while we were driving and felt that shit for myself.

Simone was a bitch that I fucked with from time to time, but she wasn't a bitch that I took serious. I had a couple of hoes that I had sex with, but that was all it was. I got a nut off, and they did too, then we went our separate ways. Simone? I had been fucking with her for the longest though. She never tried to play the main bitch role, and for that, I kept her on my roster.

Ding!

The elevator dinged, signaling that we had reached my floor, and the doors opened. There was an old white couple standing outside of the elevator doors, and they had a shocked look on their faces at the sight of Simone's hands still in my pants. I shot them a smirk, even though I wanted to bust out laughing at the pale, flushed expressions on their faces.

"Chill, ma," I spoke, and just like that, she straightened up.

Taking her hands from my pants, she turned around and strolled off of the elevator like it was nothing. I walked behind her and nodded my head toward the couple.

"Enjoy your night."

Simone strutted down the hallway, letting her dress rise above her hips, not giving a fuck who saw. She was too drunk. The dress was way too short and way too tight for her thick ass thighs, but she had worn it anyway. These hoes were all the same; they wanted to have all eyes on them in the club, and the way they did that was to wear basically nothing when going out. Shit, they were going to be naked, and me as a nigga, I was definitely going to look.

Simone stopped in front of my door, waiting for me to unlock it. Putting my hand on the door, it scanned my hand as it used my handprint to unlock it. I wasn't with that key shit because people could easily get a copy of your key and be up in ya shit. The only way a muthafucka could get into my shit was if they were to cut off my right hand, and I doubted anybody would be bold enough to do that.

The door beeped, and I pushed it open. Walking in first, I flipped the switch on my right-hand side, and instantly, my whole condo lit up. That was another thing I had done. I didn't want to ever walk into my shit and there were any surprises if anybody miraculously got through my door, so I had my shit set up that this one switch could light up the entire condo so that I could see everything. I was a paranoid nigga, but I definitely had a reason to be.

Simone walked in right behind me, and I closed the door behind us. As soon as I turned around, she was already on her knees. I stood in place as she unbuckled my belt and pulled down the black jeans that I had on. My dick was already a little hard from the way she was rubbing on my shit on the elevator. She pulled down my Ethika briefs, and my dick popped out like a jack in the box.

Looking up at me, Simone licked her lips and started to jack my dick with one hand.

"Stop playing with that shit," I ordered.

I didn't need all that damn foreplay. All I needed was my dick fucked and sucked 'cause between that bottle of Belaire and the sour I had smoked, a nigga's head was gone. I stepped out of my jeans. Standing up from her knees, Simone grabbed my hand and led me over to the couch. I sat down on the black leather sofa, and she wasted no time taking off the dress that she was wearing. Taking off the shirt I was wearing, I sat back.

Simone climbed on top of me and straddled me with both of her legs on either side of me. Leaning forward, she grabbed my dick with her right hand, but I grabbed her arm and stopped her.

"Now you know I'm not hitting nothing raw. Go grab a condom from the pocket of my jeans."

She rolled her eyes up into her head as if she was annoyed, but her ass listened and got up to go and get the condom like I told her. Walking back over to me, she opened the condom and slid it over my dick. Once it was covered, she got on me and slid down on my tool. Her pussy grabbed my dick, but it wasn't tight at all. I didn't know if she had already fucked tonight or what, but this pussy was so fucking loose.

Bouncing up and down, she tried to pull all the stops, riding me like a cowgirl, but the shit just wasn't working. Her arms were wrapped around my neck as she grinded her hips and rode my dick. Usually, this shit would be feeling great, but tonight, this shit was all wrong. This was not the birthday pussy a nigga should have been receiving.

"Yo, get up," I ordered as I tapped her thigh.

"Get up?" she asked with her eyes narrowed.

"Man, just get up. I'm not in the mood no more."

She stood up, and my condom covered dick was now limp. That wack, loose ass pussy had fucked up my whole mood, and a nigga wasn't even horny anymore.

"Damn, it's like that?" Simone looked at my dick and noticed that he wasn't speaking the same language that he was just a little while ago.

"Yeah. My head just not in it," I said, trying to save her the embarrassment of the truth. "You need me to get you an Uber?" I was only offering because she had ridden over with me from the club, and I didn't want her to think she was spending the night. She might have been at my crib a couple of times, but I wasn't about to let her spend the night.

"Nah, I'm good. I don't need a limp dick ass nigga that can't even fucking perform to do anything for me. You couldn't even fuck me, so what I need with you?"

Chuckling, I put my hands together in front of my chin as if I was praying. This bitch was trying me, and she had never done this before, so I didn't understand why tonight was different. It had to be the liquor giving her courage that she usually didn't have. I didn't take disrespect from anyone, and the shit that she had just said to me was so disrespectful that there was fire burning in my eyes. She was lucky if I didn't choke her ass until she turned blue.

Standing up from the couch, I pulled the condom from my dick and walked up to Simone and slapped her ass with it. Simone was lucky that I didn't put my hands on women.

"Bitch, when the fuck you ever known me not to be able to perform? That loose goose ass pussy is the fucking problem. Put on that cheap ass dress you can barely fucking fit, and get the fuck out of my crib before I kill yo' ass, because it seems like you forgot who the fuck you talking to!" My voice boomed through the condo. "And take that fucking waste of a condom with you!"

Simone was now wearing a scared expression on her face. Picking up her dress, she put it over her arm and scurried to the door and out of my condo. Her ass was butt ass naked walking into the hallway, but if she knew like I knew, that was safer than being around me for another minute. Shaking my head, I walked toward the bathroom so I could shower.

I could easily call up another bitch to have sex with, but I didn't show anyone where I lived. Simone only knew where I lived because I had been fucking with her for a while. Going into the bathroom, I started the shower. A nigga was ready to just chill, get high, and listen to some music before I fell out. Music was my getaway.

Some people liked to watch TV, but I loved to listen to music and just vibe out. I especially loved the music that took me to a whole other world while I listened to it. The water was nice and warm, just how I liked it. Getting into the shower, I stood under the water as it rolled down my bare chest. My thoughts wandered to Grei.

Her ass was bad as fuck, and I didn't give a damn that she was Tommy's bitch. I wasn't one to throw salt on a nigga, but his bitch was feeling me, and I was going to make that happen. The way she was staring at me from across the club and the way her body shuddered under my scrutiny, I knew she was feeling me. Only thing that was stopping me from getting at her was that we hadn't had a chance alone yet.

I wasn't a thirsty nigga though, so I was just going to wait and see what the fuck happened. Lathering up my washcloth, I washed myself from head to toe. It was a damn shame that Simone's pussy had ruined my damn night and nut like that. Her shit had never felt like that before, and I definitely wasn't going to be fucking with her ass again. If a bitch could fuck two niggas back to back, you never knew what a trifling bitch like that was capable of.

Rinsing off, I turned the shower off then opened the shower door and grabbed my towel from the towel rack. I started with my wet face then dried the rest of my body. Stepping out of the shower, I stood on the rug for a minute as I used my towel to dry my legs and feet. Walking out of the bathroom, turning off the light, I headed upstairs to my room and opened the top drawer, taking out a pair of briefs and put them on.

My room was about the same size as the living room. This condo had a lot of open space, and that was one thing I loved about it. I had a lot of money, and I could easily buy a house, but shit, it was just me, and a condo was more realistic for me. I had a California king-sized bed that was lifted a bit off the ground. I had a huge entertainment center with a sixty-five-inch TV and a stereo system.

Walking to the entertainment center, I hit the power button, and instantly, the sounds of Nas came through the speakers. I didn't listen to these new niggas much because I liked good, authentic music. Nas was one of my favorite artists because I loved the way he spit, and when you listened to his music, it was like watching a movie. You could picture everything that he was saying.

> *How can I trust you when I can't trust me?*
> *Picture myself a old man, a O.G.*
> *Some niggas will conversate with liars all day*
> *Time pass (Nah, let me start somethin' else)*
> *Soul on ice, death threats given by clowns*
> *I guess livin' is prison when you live around clowns*
> *I'm hexed, cursed, worse I been blessed first*

Bobbing my head to the music, I walked over to my nightstand and opened the top drawer. Pulling out my trippy kit as I called it, I opened the box where I kept my weed and pulled out that and a Dutch. Sitting on my bed, I chilled and listened to the music as I rolled up. Once I was done rolling up, I put the box on top of my nightstand because I knew I would probably be smoking again tonight.

Getting up from the bed, I turned the light off, and now, the only light in the room came from the lit stereo and the lights from outside coming in through the window. My condo was downtown, so there was always something lit up. Lying in bed on my back, I grabbed the lighter from the nightstand and lit the blunt. The sour invaded my lungs as I inhaled and exhaled. This was why I loved having my own shit and my own space. It was nothing like relaxing with a blunt, my thoughts, and some dope ass rhymes. Happy birthday to a real nigga.

TOMMY BANKS

*S*itting in my office, I was still dressed in the suit that I wore to the party. My jacket was off, and my tie and shirt were undone, but I was still dressed. I downed the Hennessy that was in my snifter and slammed the glass down so hard that it almost broke. Grei was my heart, but she was such a disrespectful bitch. What did she think? That I hadn't noticed the way she would stare at Knight any time we were around his ass like I wasn't in the room?

It was like she got in front of his ass and forgot just who in the fuck she was with. She forgot that I would slap her into the next day for even the slightest disrespect. Opening the china canister that I had on my desk, I pulled out a vial of some of the finest coke. Lining it up on the desk, I snorted it and instantly felt the high as it rushed to my head.

The more I thought about it, the more pissed off I became. The whole ride home, we rode in silence, and I was trying to not put my hands on Grei, but it was becoming harder and harder. I hated having to show her the demon that was inside of me, but she could never just be obedient and be a good bitch. Getting up from my seat, I walked over to the bar with my glass in hand and refilled it. I shot it back without even putting the top back on the bottle of liquor. Putting the glass down beside it, I exited my office and walked upstairs toward the bedroom in search of Grei.

Getting closer to the room, I could hear water running, and I knew that she was taking a shower. Walking into the bathroom, the dress that she had worn was thrown on the floor like it didn't cost a grip. When I first got involved with Grei, she was nothing but a naïve girl that knew nothing about labels and designer. You could give her a hundred dollars and she would go and find a whole outfit with that. Now, I had her accustomed to the finer things in life, but it was like she didn't even appreciate the shit. She'd rather wear something from Forever 21 and shit like that.

I showered her with gifts, and although I put my hands on her a bit, it was nothing compared to the love I showed her. In my eyes, she was getting off easy, and she needed to appreciate me for that. Our bathroom was gold and white; she had decorated it herself. Our sink, toilet, and accessories were gold, and the wall was white with a gold diamond pattern on it. The shower doors were glass and see-through, but they were lightly frosted gold.

She didn't even realize that I was in the room with her as she stood under the water, letting it flow down her body. Her breasts were big and voluptuous; she sported a tiny waist, and her ass was fat. The shit was all natural, and she wasn't even a person that worked out like crazy to have a banging ass body. My dick wanted to defy me and get hard, and the coke that I had flowing through my veins was making me even more horny.

I wanted to curse her out and slap her a little bit for the little show she had put on in the club, but then I wanted to bend her over and fuck the shit out of her. Taking off my clothes, I started to strip right there, letting my pants and boxers fall to the ground and pulling my arms out of my shirt. In less than ten seconds, I was as naked as the day that I was born. Sliding the glass door open, Grei jumped as she tried to cover herself up.

"Fuck you doing that for? It could only be me," I spoke as I got into the shower.

"It was just a reflex; my bad," she replied as she turned back around toward the water.

Reaching over her, I grabbed my towel and my bottle of Dove Men's body wash. We didn't talk as she washed up, and I did the same, but her ample ass was on my mind the entire time. Once I was done washing off, I used the shower head that we had in the back and rinsed off. Our shower was equipped with two shower heads, one in the front and one in the back so that we could take showers together. This was something that was far and in between though because we rarely took showers together anymore.

Putting my towel back up, I went ahead and wrapped my arms around Grei's waist, and I felt her body tense a little, but then she tried to relax it again. My blood boiled at the fact that she hated when I touched her, even in an intimate moment like this. Trying to ignore the way her body reacted to me, I gripped her stomach and started to place kisses on her neck. My dick was hard as a brick as it poked into her backside.

Grei was silent; not a moan or anything escaped from her lips.

"Bend over," I whispered into her ear as I stuck my tongue out and licked her lobe.

Grei turned off the water and bent over, placing her hands on the knobs for leverage. Grabbing her by her waist, I pushed my dick inside of her pussy and bit my bottom lip. Her shit was so wet and tight; it always had been. The shit was something like an addiction, and there was no way I was going to let another nigga get a piece of this.

Pounding into her, she started to moan finally, but I wanted that shit louder.

Whap, whap!

I slapped her ass, and it started to jiggle uncontrollably. Her pussy was becoming wetter as I pounded in and out of her. Grei removed one hand from the knob, reached under, and started to massage my balls. Throwing my head back, I relished in the moment as I felt myself about to come.

"Shit!" I yelled out as I came, and my pounding came to a stop. "Damn."

Pulling my dick out, I turned around to the shower head that was by me and washed my dick off again. Grei turned hers on and washed up as well without talking, then got out before I was even done. Shaking my head, I cracked my knuckles as I tried to think of anything else but beating her ass. It wasn't working though.

Turning the water off, I opened the shower door and grabbed a towel and started to dry myself off as I walked into our room. Grei was standing at her nightstand, popping a plan B. Yeah, that was the last fucking straw.

"Yo, what the fuck are you doing?"

"Huh?" she asked with an uncertain tone.

"Why the fuck you over there popping pills right after I fucking nut in you? What, you too good to have a nigga's baby?" My voice boomed as beads of sweat started to appear on my head.

"Tommy, are you high? You must be high because I didn't say or do anything for you to be yelling," she responded as she shook her head side to side, almost as if she was bothered by me. That was another thing. Any time I said something to her, she wanted to blame it on me being high. Nah, it was because she liked to test me like I was some weak ass nigga.

"Grei," I started, "I'm trying so hard not to put my hands on yo' ass, but you're making it real fucking hard with that slick ass mouth you got." I looked at her with a look in my eyes, letting her know what time it was and that I was not in the damn mood.

"Okay. I'm popping a morning after pill so that I won't get pregnant."

"I know what the fuck you're doing, but why? You my bitch, and I have money, so why can't we have a baby?"

I was confused why she didn't want to have a kid with a nigga. When we first started dating, I would ask her if she wanted kids, and she assured me that she did. When I would joke about having kids with me, her ass would blush, but now if I nutted in her, she would pop a morning after pill like it was a Skittle, even though I already allowed her to be on birth control pills.

"Money just isn't everything, Tommy. Look at the way we argue and the way you're always mad, threatening me, and putting your hands on me. The way you snort coke like it's powdered candy. A baby?" She chuckled. "We're not ready for that."

Nodding my head up and down, my tongue explored my mouth as I sucked my teeth. Turning my back to her, I walked over to our dresser and opened the second drawer, pulling out a pair of boxers, and put them on. Grei walked up next to me and opened the top drawer, pulling out a pair of her boy shorts and a sports bra. She closed the drawer back and went to walk back to the bed, but I caught her by the long ass bundles in her head—the ones I had paid for.

Pulling her close to me, her head snapped back, and her body went stiff. I knew she didn't expect for me to react to what she said because I had turned around as if it was nothing, but I wasn't about to let her ass off the hook tonight.

"You got so much fucking mouth until a nigga put his hands on you, then you the fucking victim."

Mushing the back of her head, I pushed her down, and she fell onto the hardwood floor. Swiftly walking into our walk-in closet, I grabbed my red Gucci belt that I had hanging on the wall. Grei must have thought I was done because she was getting up from the floor. Her back was to me.

Whap!

I slapped her across the ass with the belt.

"Ahhh!" she screamed as she turned around and looked at me in horror.

The look on her face didn't mean shit as I continued to hit her with the belt.

Whap!

I hit her across her stomach, and instantly, a welt appeared.

Whip, whip!

Whap!

I hit her across her thighs.

"Stop, Tommy! Please!"

There were tears running down her face as she turned around and hurried to hop in the bed and cover her body, but I followed behind her, hitting her across the back. I put as much strength as I could into it because I needed her to understand to stop fucking playing with me. Once she was in the bed, she pulled the thick cover over her and put it over herself as if it were a shield. I thought about pulling it back and hitting her a couple more times, but a nigga's arm was getting tired.

"This time, it's a belt. If I have to deal with ya mouth like a fucking kid, I'mma beat ya ass like I raised you every fucking time. Throw all them fucking pills out 'cause if I want ya stanking ass to have my baby, that's just what the fuck you gonna do. I pay for everything around this bitch, and what the fuck I say goes. You think you make decisions around this bitch!" I yelled, and she shook her head no. "Exactly. Stay in ya fucking place, Grei, and the next time I catch you eyeing any nigga, I'mma beat you so fucking bad ya momma gon' feel it, bitch."

Dropping the belt on the floor, I turned around and walked toward the door. Pausing, I turned the light off.

"Goodnight. By the time I get back, ya ass better be sleep or silent as fuck because I don't wanna hear all that bullshit ass crying."

Walking away, I headed back to my office. I was about to have my own lil' party with my white girl and my brown liquor. Shit, I might even dip out and go fuck a bitch.

GREI

*A*fter Tommy beat me like I was a kid that talked back to their parent, he left me in the room to sleep. I didn't know why I didn't try to hit him back, but it was like every time he started to hit me, I just cowered. I didn't know if it was the coke or not, but last night, his eyes were so red that it looked like the devil was dancing in them. His pupils were dilated, and I was afraid that if I ever fought him back that he would try to really kill me.

I was lying in bed, looking at the ceiling, wondering why did I get myself into a relationship with someone like him. I had morals; my parents taught me how to respect myself. My father never laid a hand on my mother, and he rarely raised his voice when it came to her. Even though my father was strict, he was great, and if he knew what Tommy was doing to me, I was sure he would try and kill him. No, he *would* kill him.

Before Tommy left out of bed this morning, he told me that we were having company tonight, and I was to make dinner. He made sure to tell me not to make any of my Nigerian food and that I needed to make American food. He loved to brag about how he was Dominican, but when I tried to show my culture, there was always a problem, almost like he was ashamed of where I had come from. Getting up from the bed, I walked as light as possible to the bathroom because my body was feeling sore.

The light from the window outside shined so bright that I didn't need to turn the light on as I looked in the mirror. There were bruises and welts all over my torso, and when I turned around, on the back of my legs. On my back, there were dark bruises that were still healing from the last time he beat my ass. Tears threatened to pour out of my eyes as I looked at myself; I mean *really* looked at myself.

I was beautiful on the outside and inside and was letting this no good, drug using coward destroy that. He was destroying me, and if I stayed any longer, he would succeed in destroying me altogether. Shaking my head, I started the shower so that I could get myself together to head out to the grocery store. Last night, when Tommy joined me in the shower, I swear my skin was crawling. I didn't even want to have sex with him, but I had denied him sex before, and that didn't turn out too good.

Sex with Tommy used to be good, but it was never great. To be honest, his dick was so small that I could barely feel much, but it was like I loved him so much that it didn't matter. Now, I had little to no feelings for him, and it felt like he was aimlessly drilling into me. Something had to give because I was growing so tired of this shit.

Getting into the shower, I washed up and started to get myself together. My mind wandered to Knight. I didn't even know that Tommy noticed how I was looking at him, and if he did, then maybe Knight noticed too. I was sorry, but I couldn't help it. He was just that sexy with this swag to die for. I didn't know if Tommy really beat me for my mouth, birth control, or because I had looked at Knight like he was a full-course meal; maybe it was all three.

"Oh well," I said aloud to myself as I turned the water off and opened the glass shower door.

Grabbing my towel, I dried my feet as I got out and stood on the gold rug that was right outside of the tub. I finished drying my body then stood at the sink as I brushed my teeth and washed my face. My sew-in was still intact, even though Tommy yanked my bundles so hard that he could have pulled a track out, so I just used my wig brush and brushed it to pull the kinks out. I picked up a hair tie from the countertop and pulled my hair into a low ponytail.

Walking into the room, I went into the walk-in closet and searched for something to wear. I was just running to the grocery store, so it didn't need to be anything fancy, but I still wanted to look cute. I decided on a pair of high-waist denim shorts and a navy blue and white Tommy Hilfiger shirt with my matching slides. It was a really cute on-the-go kind of outfit. The welts on my legs were at the top of my thighs, so they were covered by the shorts.

Exiting the closet, clothes in hand, I sat on the edge of my bed and grabbed my lotion from my nightstand as I started to lotion my legs, starting from my thighs and down. Tommy was out for the day but assured me that he would be home for dinner, even though I had never asked. Shit, if he and his company went out for dinner instead of coming here, that would be okay by me, and I didn't even know who was coming. Finally dressed, I grabbed my purse and headed downstairs and out of the door.

> Get money, go hard, damn fuckin' right
> Stunt on these bitches out of mothafuckin' spite
> Ain't no runnin' up on me, went from nothin' to glory
> I ain't tellin' y'all to do it, I'm just tellin' my story
> I don't hang with these bitches cause these bitches
>   be corny
> And I got enough bras, y'all ain't gotta support me

Every time I listened to this song, the shit made me want to cry. It made me think of when I was young, and my father used to struggle to make ends meet. I didn't have the latest fashion, so getting teased was the norm for me. I became accustomed to the shit, but it still hurt deep down inside.

Now look at me. I had everything that anyone could want, but I wasn't happy. The materialistic shit didn't mean anything when I wasn't happy within, and being with Tommy wasn't making me happy at all. Getting out of my thoughts, I changed the song and "Bickenhead" blared through the speakers. Pulling into the parking lot of Wegmans, I found a close spot then got out and locked the doors to my all-white 2018 Audi and made my way into the store.

Once I was in the store, I grabbed a shopping cart, pulled my phone from my purse, and opened the Notes app. I had made a grocery list before leaving the house so that I could remember everything to get from the store. The last thing I felt like doing was having to make two trips because I forgot something that I needed. The meal I decided to make tonight was fried chicken wings, baked chicken thighs, yellow rice, fried cabbage, and blueberry muffins.

Walking around the packed store, I found everything I needed and then headed to the line to check out. The line went surprisingly fast for it to be the beginning of the month. Walking outside, I noticed a table set up with a young lady that was selling books. Immediately, my interests were piqued. Looking at the table, her books looked just like the ones I would read. Urban fiction; the books with men you wished you knew in real life and women that you just wanted to win.

"How much are they?" I asked her.

"Hello, they're all ten dollars each," she responded with a smile.

To me, that was a steal, and it had been a while since I could sit and read a good book. There was always somewhere Tommy wanted me to go or something he needed cleaned or cooked; it was basically like raising a child, being in a relationship with him. I was all for catering to a man but when he deserved it. This shit was like a job I was forced to do, because I didn't even want to be with his ass.

Buying a three-part series, I left from the store now satisfied that I had something to read tonight. The drive back home was only about a ten-minute drive, so I was back home in no time. I let out a sigh of relief when I saw that Tommy still was gone. I was happy for that because I hated when he would stand over my shoulder while I cooked. Parking in our mini parking lot, I cut the engine then grabbed the bags and got out.

I didn't know what time we were expecting company, but I needed to get dinner started now. Opening the front door, I walked into the empty, quiet house. I remember when I first moved in here. I was so damn in love with this house when Tommy first brought me here. He showed it to me and two weeks later was asking if I could move in with him. Of course, my dumb ass said yeah and moved in.

Before, I used to be so happy when I lived here because it was beautiful and just gave me a homey feeling. I didn't know if it was because the love was no longer there for the house or between Tommy and I, but when I walked in now, my soul cringed, and the hairs on the back of my neck stood up. Walking into the kitchen, I dropped the bags down on the counter then put my purse on the back of a chair.

Pulling my phone from my purse, I unlocked it and turned on my music. Music could always get me through a cooking session. Taking all of the groceries from the bag, I laid them down on the counter. When I cooked, I always loved to see everything out in front of me.

You ain't the only one, who can turn your phone off
  Baby I know how to press ignore, I won't be crying anymore
  You ain't the only one, you ain't the only one who can be a show off
  This body look good, out on the town, so many boys wanna be down
  You ain't the only one

THE SOUNDS of Tammy Rivera blasted through the kitchen as I sang along to the words. I loved her album; it was something like a hidden jewel. I really thought that singers made the best music when they were going through something. The chicken thighs were in the oven, the oil on the stove was nice and hot, rice was on, and the bacon was in the pan cooking for the cabbage.

The kitchen was smelling good already. That was one thing that I knew how to do, and that was cook. My mother made sure of that from a young age, that I knew how to cook. She would have me in the kitchen with her, whether it was a big meal to a small one; there I was, helping.

Once everything was started and there was nothing for me to do except mix the blueberry muffin batter, I sat at the wooden kitchen table. Pulling out my phone, I started scrolling through Instagram. While I was on there, the blue notification in the top right corner of my screen lit up and displayed a number '1', letting me know that I had a DM.

Opening it, there was a message displayed from Farah.

Hey cousin. It was great seeing you, and even though we're not as close as we used to be I just wanted to tell you that I love you. If you ever need anything, just call or text me.

After reading the message, I made sure to send her a message back, letting her know I loved her too. It was so crazy how close we used to be, almost like sisters, and now we were just two people that lived in the same city. Closing my phone, I thought about how my life had changed from being with this man. I was no longer the happy Grei that was always in a good mood.

Most days, I was down and depressed. I rarely left the house unless I was with Tommy, and I hated those moments. I knew that I needed to get out of here because he was slowly but surely draining my spirit from me. It was just going to be hard leaving everything that I knew and really, everything that I had.

KNIGHT

Is you fuckin'? (Yeah) Baby girl I need to know (who?)
Who finna run get the rubbers from the store?
   (Who there?)
Bitch so damn wet, drippin' on my marble floor (drip,
   drip, drip)
Never not strapped, in my city, on my foe
Pull up in a two-seater (yeah,) in a wife-beater

I normally didn't listen to these new niggas, but this song was actually fire. Puffing on a blunt, I headed to this nigga Tommy's house. We always had monthly meetings, but this was the first time that we would be having it at his house. Apparently, he was having his fine ass woman make us dinner or some shit. I didn't know why that nigga was trying to kiss my ass, but I was sure about to see.

Tommy asked me to be at his crib around six, but shit, that was too early to eat, so I was getting there around seven. Pulling up to his crib, I could do nothing but shake my head at this nigga's house. I knew he was a flashy type of nigga, but this was just too much. The black iron gate stopped me from entering the premises.

Just as I was about to roll my window down to push the red button on the intercom, the gates started to open. His ass must have been waiting for a nigga's arrival. Pulling in, I took note of the premises. There was a lot of land on the side of the house, and I would imagine the back had just as much space. The driveway was large, and there were four cars parked.

The house was huge. It was a white mini-mansion with large white pillars in the front. Pulling next to a black Rolls Royce, I cut the engine and took one last pull from the blunt then put it in the ashtray. Getting out, I checked my hip to make sure my gun was on my waist, then I headed to the door. You could never be too careful around niggas. I was dressed casually in a pair of white Levi jeans with a red and white Levi shirt. On my feet was a pair of white Gucci sneakers with the green and red lines on the side.

Ding, Dong!

The sound of the doorbell filled my ears just as I hit the red illuminating button that was on the side of the door. I waited about twenty seconds before the door opened.

"Damn," slipped out of my mouth.

"Hi. I'm Grei." She stuck her hand out to introduce herself.

Tommy and I had been doing business for years, but he never let anyone get close to Grei. Grei was his prized possession, and he probably knew if she ever got a sniff of a real nigga that her ass would be gone; and if it was up to me, then she would be.

Taking her hand, I shook it softly but made sure to hold it for a moment as I stepped into the house.

"Knight. Nice to meet you." Looking her up and down, I bit my bottom lip as I stroked her arm. She was looking good as fuck in a yellow off the shoulder dress that stopped below her ass. It covered it, so I couldn't see her ass, but it still left little to the imagination. She had a simple pair of yellow sandals on her feet.

The color looked good against her chocolate skin, making her even more beautiful. Her hair was bone straight with a part in the middle just like she had it at my party. Grei's eyes looked dark, not in a bad way, but like she had the eyeliner shit on. The shape of her eyes was sexy as hell, and I could just picture sliding her dress up and sliding my dick inside her thick ass.

"What's up, man?" Tommy came walking down the stairs, looking like a damn clown.

Grei pulled her arm away from me, and I smiled at her. This nigga Tommy walked over and slapped me up like he didn't know I was down here getting ready to finesse his bitch. Tommy was wearing a purple silk shirt with a pair of black pants and a pair of black Clark loafers on his feet. The silk shirt was tucked in and was open a bit in the front.

I didn't know why that nigga was dressed like he was about to go dance to some salsa, or like he was some Escobar type of drug dealer. This nigga was trying to put on some fucking show, and it better had been for his bitch and not for me. He knew the type of nigga I was, and none of this shit impressed me. Maybe he was trying to prove some shit, but then again, this nigga was really just a fucking clown.

"What's up, man?" I put my hand out to dap him up, even though he had his arms open, trying to embrace me. He took the hint quick and dapped me up.

"Dinner is already done," Grei said as she closed the door.

"Shit. I forgot something upstairs," Tommy said as he patted his pockets in search of whatever it was he had left upstairs. "Grei, show him to the dining room table." He headed upstairs, and I looked at Grei, waiting for baby girl to lead the way.

"This way." She walked straight ahead, and I followed behind her, watching her ass on the way.

"You look good as hell in this dress," I complimented her as she walked.

"Umm, thanks."

"What you confused about?"

"I didn't say I was confused." She looked back with her eyebrows dipped.

"Saying umm is a sign of confusion. So again, what are you confused about?"

We reached the dining room that was already set with three places.

The table was long. It had three chairs on each side then a chair on each end. There was a place set at each end then on the left of one of the ends. That must have been for Tommy, and Grei's seat was next to him. I wanted to be an asshole and sit in his seat, but I wasn't going to disrespect and bitch his ass in his own home.

"For the record," Grei started as I sat down, "I'm not confused about anything, just taken aback since you're complimenting a man's wife that you work for."

Turning around, she walked away as if she had proved a point, but little did her ass know, she hadn't done shit. Even more, what she said was false. Sitting down, I took a look around the dining room. It was cool, but it seemed like a damn model home. There were no pictures hanging on walls or no shit like that.

The dining room was painted white, and there were a couple of abstract paintings on the wall. There was a bar over to the right of the room that held everything from wine to liquor and even a couple bottles of champagne. One day I would buy a house. I wouldn't overdo it with shit that didn't matter though, but my shit was going to be nice. This big ass house was some shit that I wanted to do when I started a family. To me, that was just more logical than to do it as a bachelor.

Looking at my hands, I realized that I needed to wash them before eating. Money had been in and out of my hands all day, and there was no telling what the hell was on it. Getting up from the table, I went in search of Grei to see where the bathroom was. The sound of my shoes resonated against the marble floors. Walking through the living room, I didn't see her, so I continued my journey.

The house was set up with two different hallways sprouting from the main foyer. Reaching the foyer, my eye bounced around the room. When I walked in before, I hadn't paid attention to the way it looked, and now that I did, I knew exactly what it reminded me of. It was white and gold with a large winding staircase. There was the same statue from Scarface that read 'The World Is Yours.'

Yeah, this nigga thought he was some big-time nigga. Heading down the other hallway, the smell of food was hitting my nose. I smelled it before, but the closer I got, a nigga's stomach started growling. The kitchen was empty, so walking on, I saw a closed door that I assumed was the bathroom. With a house this damn big, there'd better be a bathroom on each floor; shit, in each wing.

It was a white door with a gold circular doorknob. Turning the knob and pushing the door open, my insides immediately got hot. There was Grei, standing at the vanity with her dress pulled up, looking at the fresh marks and bruises on her skin. Grei was chocolate, but she was like a milk chocolate, so you could still see the marks on her skin. You could tell they were fresh because there were welts, and those usually didn't last that long.

"Who the fuck did that to you?" My voice boomed, even though I didn't mean for it to. This wasn't my bitch, but for some reason, seeing those bruises on that beautiful skin was fucking with me.

Grei was pulling her dress down to cover her exposed, bruised thigh. It was too late though, because I had already seen it, and I needed answers. I didn't give a fuck that I had invaded her privacy in this bathroom.

"Tommy, but it was a mistake."

She was defending him, even though I knew this wasn't a damn mistake. That only meant one thing. That this was something that he did on a regular basis and not no one time shit. Baby girl was in here getting fucked up by this nigga, yet she was defending him.

"You're too fucking beautiful for this yo. Never let no man put they damn hands on you."

Finally, I closed the door and went in search of Tommy. I didn't give a fuck that it was his house or his bitch right now. I wasn't a fan of that beating on a woman shit. Down the hallway and then up the stairs, there were five doors, and they were all closed except one. It didn't take a genius to know what room he was in. Without knocking, I opened the door that was closed.

This nigga Tommy was bent over, sniffing product like it was candy. I didn't know this nigga even did coke. If I did, I damn sure wouldn't have put him in charge of my operation. I would never let the nigga even act like a boss if that was the case.

"Oh shit, man. What's up? I was just coming down." He stood up from the desk he was sitting behind and started to straighten out his pants and brush them off, even though there was nothing on them. This nigga was tweaking.

"Oh, word? After you finished getting high then, huh? Talking about you forgot something. What, you forgot to snort that shit up ya nose, nigga?" My face was twisted, and there was a menacing look in my eyes.

I was mad as fuck for more reasons than one. The first was the real reason I bum rushed into his office in the first place. The second was what the nigga was doing in his office. The first rule to the game was supposed to be obeyed no matter what, and that was to never get high on your own supply.

How could we supply coke and crack if this nigga was snorting it up his damn nose? I didn't care if it was twenty dollars' worth; it was taking away from what we could be making, and he was creating a deadly habit. A habit that could potentially ruin my empire, no matter how small the habit was now.

"It's not even like that, man. This shit ain't nothing. I don't even do this shit all the time," he started explaining.

"Nah, nigga. If you gotta get high before having a meeting where ya head need to be clear, then you have a problem. And I wasn't aware that you had a fucking problem with your hands either."

"A problem with my hands?"

"If you can repeat what the fuck I said, then you can answer the question. Tommy, on some real shit, my nigga, I'm liable to blow ya fucking brains out right now because I feel like you playing with my fucking intelligence." Raising my shirt, I displayed the gun tucked in my waist that he should have already known I had.

Tommy knew just what type of nigga I was. I didn't fake crazy; a nigga was really crazy and would kill his ass and not give a fuck. He knew that. His hands were up in surrender as he started trying to plead his case.

"I re-really have no idea w-what you talking about, man. I know you mad about this coke shit, and I will leave that shit alone, but my

32

hands to myself? Man, I don't know what you talking about." He was talking so fast that he was stumbling over his words.

"Grei. You put your hands on that woman like a fucking coward." My tone was calm. It always was when I was ready to kill a nigga.

"She told you that?" His eyebrows were pushed together like he just couldn't believe that she would tell someone.

"She didn't tell me shit. I saw the bruises on her legs. You the only muthafucka that could have did that shit to that girl. You beat women now, nigga?"

"No, no, man. It was a one-time thing. I was off that shit, and, man..."

He stopped speaking as I walked up on him. I was face to face and toe to toe with the nigga. Tommy was shaking like a stripper at a church, even though he was trying to stay cool. I could tell by the way he kept his chin down and refused to not look me in the eye.

I laughed and backed away because I could at least respect a nigga that didn't go out like no bitch.

"I see a nigga got some heart, so I'm not going to kill you. Keep ya hands off her ass, man, because if I see so much as a papercut on her, I'm going to kill you, and that's a promise. Now, I know this was supposed to be a meeting, but I really don't feel like dealing with ya ass. Am I losing money?"

"No. Money still coming in like clockwork." He told me what I already knew. I may have stayed in the background because I didn't like being all flashy and muthafuckas knowing who I was, but I stayed up on my own empire and knew everything."

"Aight then. I'm out."

Turning around, I went down the stairs and out the door. I didn't even check on baby girl because I already told her what I needed to say, and if she wanted to stay and accept that from that no-good ass nigga, then what could I do? People, especially women, always did what the fuck they wanted to do.

GREI

*A*s soon as I heard the front door close, I ran to the room that held all of my clothes and started to fill my luggage with clothes. Tommy was leaving to go to Dominican Republic, and usually, he would make me go, but I was relieved that he didn't this time. Why? I didn't know, but I didn't care to ask or mention it. I pulled dresses, jeans, and shirts from the hangers, shoes from the floor, and threw them in my opened Louis Vuitton luggage.

After I got as much as I could from the closet, I closed my suitcase and grabbed my duffle bag. Going to the dresser, I filled the duffle bag up with panties, bras, socks, and my hygiene products, and things that I just couldn't live without, like my Gucci and YSL perfume. I was already dressed in a pair of black leggings and a black tank top. Going over to the other side of my dresser, I put my whole jewelry box into my bag as well.

That conversation with Knight, the other night when I made dinner, had opened my eyes. I mean, I already knew that this relationship was horrible, of course, but having someone see me like that and feel bad for me, made me feel like shit. Tommy should have been feeling like shit, not me, but here I was, yet again, blaming myself.

Blaming myself for doing something to piss him off, but then I blamed myself for not fighting back.

There was no more blaming myself, and I wasn't staying here anymore. Tommy didn't know my worth, but I did, and the shit was going to stop now. After closing up my luggage, I looked around the room to make sure there was nothing that I was leaving. Tears threatened to pour out of my eyes as I thought about all the memories we shared here. Not the bad ones but the good ones.

Shaking my head, I wiped my eyes, picked up my bags, and walked out of the room, down the stairs, and out of the house. I was done with him, and I was ready to start my life without him and all his bullshit.

After all of the times that we tried
I found out we were living a lie
And after all of this love that we made
I know now you don't love me the same
The way that I love
The way that I love
The way that I love
(The way that I love you)

I WAS SINGING my heart out as I drove my black Audi on my way to my cousin Farah's house. We had been talking since that night she messaged me, and when I told her about my idea to leave Tommy, she offered me a place to stay in the extra room that she had. She offered it to me with no hesitation, and I appreciated that. It wasn't going to be a long-term thing, but I needed somewhere to rest my head until I found my own place.

Over the years, I started to put up money in a savings account that Tommy gave me. Shit, I had no use for new clothes because I still had shit with tags on it. Why waste that money on clothes when I could save it for something more useful in the future. Thank God for that.

Between my savings and my jewelry, if it came down to it, I was pretty much set to find a place and then find a job.

I had gotten a degree to be a dental assistant, so hopefully, that came in handy. It was one of the things Tommy did allow me to do while we were together. There were so many things going through my head at once, and I didn't know which goal to tackle. This would be my first time actually being on my own. Even though I was nervous and scared, I was also excited because I finally had the chance to live my life and be free.

It took me almost thirty minutes to get to Farah's complex because of how far out Tommy and I lived, and that was with me speeding. At first, I liked being far and out of the city, but after a while, it became more of a nuisance. I really thought he wanted me to live that far just so he could keep me hidden from people. It worked because I now had no friends, family, nothing.

Pulling into Farah's parking lot, I pulled in front of the address that I had typed into my GPS on my phone. The voice was coming through the speaker, letting me know that I had reached my destination. Parking into a spot that was nearest to her door, I unplugged my phone and called her. She answered almost immediately.

"Hello."

"Hey, I'm here."

"Really? Okay. I'm coming now to help you with your stuff."

It was almost 8 p.m., so the sun was just starting to go down. There were a couple of older kids out, but I was happy to not see any toddlers or anything out at this time. I hated to see little kids out and about when it started to get dark, especially when there weren't any parents around, which is how it usually was. The complex that Farah lived in wasn't in the hood, but it wasn't quiet either. It was a perfect mix kind of neighborhood.

After waiting a couple of minutes, Farah's door finally opened, and she came out. She was in a short ass pair of red shorts with a white spaghetti strap tank top, and I could see her pierced nipples through the material. Farah would be shunned from our family just as I had if they even saw her wearing something this provocative.

Unlocking my door, I opened it, and she embraced like she hadn't seen me in years. Technically, before running into her at the club, it actually had been years.

"Bitchhhh, I didn't think you would really leave that old bastard." She broke the hug and laughed.

"Girl, I'm sick of that old bastard," I said, mocking her. "That relationship is unhealthy, and a bitch don't need that."

"I understand, girl. Let's get your stuff out the car so I can show you your room, and we can catch up. I'm really happy you're staying here, Grei, for real. Take ya time looking for ya place and doing what you need to do. It's no rush."

There were tears in my eyes again because even after all this time, Farah was still treating me how we always treated each other—like sisters. I appreciated her for everything and couldn't wait to rekindle our relationship.

GREI

"*I* hope this place is low key like you said," I said to Farah as we drove to a bar she had been talking about.

I wasn't really in the mood to go anywhere, but I had agreed because Farah literally had asked me to go all day. She promised that it was a low-key bar, and I didn't really have to deal with any people, so that was a plus for me. The last thing I wanted to do right now was be around people, especially because there was no telling when Tommy would come looking for me.

The last couple of days had been spent in the house. I had been on Indeed looking for and applying to jobs. I hadn't got any calls back just yet, but I was confident that I would soon. I mean, I had the degree. The only thing was I never actually had a dental assistant job after getting the degree. Hopefully, that wouldn't stop potential employers from contacting me.

"It is. I swear," she responded as she swerved in and out of traffic.

Farah always drove like a bat out of hell, and if you didn't have your seat belt on as soon as you saw how she drove, you would slide that shit right on. Twenty minutes later, we were pulling up to a bar that looked almost like a little hole in the wall, but it was in the college town area that would get crowded with college kids. Don't get me wrong; I loved partying with the white people, but tonight, I just wasn't going for all that. The parking lot was empty though, which was a good sign.

Farah parked in the spot that was right by the door and cut the engine.

"You ready?"

Sighing, I replied, "Yeah, I guess."

We got out of the car and walked into the bar with Farah in the lead. We were both looking cute and casual tonight. Farah was wearing a pair of black distressed shorts with a white and black Adidas shirt that was tied in the front, and a pair of matching Adidas slides on her feet. Her hair was in the blunt cut bob that she had gotten done earlier at the salon.

I was wearing a pair of light denim, distressed high-waist jeans with a powder pink spaghetti strap shirt. On my feet were a pair of Gucci bloom supreme slides with the flowers on it, and my hair was bone straight with a part down the middle. I was also wearing a matching Gucci headband. Just like Farah said, the bar was empty besides the bartenders and a couple of patrons. We headed straight to the bar to order a drink.

"Can I get a Long Island?" Farah ordered, and the bartender nodded her head then looked at me.

"I'll take an Amaretto Sour."

"Amaretto Sour!" Farah exclaimed as if I had just ordered a drink she had never heard of before.

"What's wrong with that?" I asked her with narrowed eyes as I looked back and forth from her to the bartender that was still standing there.

"No. We're about to have a good time tonight, and an Amaretto Sour just isn't going to do. We'll take two Long Islands," she directed to the bartender that nodded her head with a smile on her face and walked away.

"Girl, you're going to have my ass drunk." I laughed.

"Good. Maybe you'll loosen up a little bit and have some fun without worrying about Tommy's wack ass."

I had been staying at Farah's house for a week, and all week long, I had been telling her about how I was nervous about Tommy finding me. She was probably tired of hearing about it, but I was just worried about what he was going to do when he came back to an empty home. This was my first time ever trying to leave him, and there was no telling how he would react. It felt like my head had been on a swivel, even though I had been in the house.

"Whatever," I replied while shaking my head.

A couple of minutes later, the bartender placed the two drinks in front of us. Now, I wasn't an expert on drinks or anything, but I could have sworn Long Islands were supposed to be brown. Ours were a light, light brown, letting me know that the shit was nothing but liquor. Already, I knew that I would be sipping on this same damn drink all night.

Taking a sip, my throat burned as if I was drinking straight liquor. Farah laughed at me as she went into her purse and handed the bartender a twenty-dollar bill.

"Farah, you're trying to kill me tonight."

"Nope, just trying to make sure you have fun." The bartender handed her back four dollars in change, but she left it on the bar for a tip.

Walking away from the bar, we walked to the back where there was a dartboard. I hadn't played darts in years, but I always loved the game, and I was ready to whoop Farah's ass in it. Maybe that would get my mind off all the bullshit that was happening in my world.

"Done whooped ya ass again!" I laughed as I took another sip of my Long Island.

Farah and I had just finished our second game, and she hadn't been able to beat me yet.

"That's that damn drink. You got like some liquor power or some shit. I have never gotten beat this bad in darts."

"You've just never played me before. That's all that is," I continued to brag.

"Whatever, hoe."

Giving the darts a rest, we sat at the back table. I got on my phone, and she did the same thing. I started to scroll through Facebook and then Instagram, but there was nothing I was really paying attention to or anything that caught my attention rather. Opening Snapchat, I decided to take some cute pictures since I was feeling this drink and myself even more.

Using filters, I made different faces as I took pictures with the dog filter and the one with flowers on my forehead. The filter that added a yellow and white flower and freckles on my face was a personal favorite, so I was taking pictures with that, when another face popped up in the camera. My heart fell into my ass as I turned around, and there stood Knight, looking sexy as he always did. He was dressed casually like he had just came out of the house to run and grab a drink real quick, just as we had.

Knight was wearing a pair of black and gray Nike basketball shorts with a black V-neck tee, and on his feet were a pair of all-black Air Max 97's. He looked like he had a fresh cut, and his waves were swimming. He had a diamond earring in both of his ears and a Rolex watch on his wrist. Knight was so damn sexy, and I had to squeeze my thighs together to stop the thumping that my clit was starting to do.

"Damn, I can't get in ya picture?" he asked as he licked his lips and looked me up and down like I was a full-course meal. Shit, I was though.

"I didn't say that, but I didn't know who you were, hopping in my picture," I responded with a smile on my face.

"Well, now you know who a nigga is, so let's take a picture together. And don't use one of those gay ass flower shits either."

Laughing, I opened my phone, and we took a couple of pictures with no filter at all. All the damn filters were girlie, so we really had no other choice.

"Dang, y'all snapping it up like y'all a whole couple over there, and, Grei, you haven't even introduced him to your favorite cousin," Farah spoke up, taking a sip from her Long Island.

Honestly, I was so into what Knight and I were doing that I had almost forgotten that she was across the table from us. He had that type of aura about him. I was captured, and nothing else around me even mattered.

"My bad." I laughed. "Knight, this is my cousin, Farah. Farah, this is Knight."

He nodded at her to acknowledge her, and she said hi.

Buzz, buzz.

Farah picked up her vibrating phone from the table and answered it with her professional voice on. It was so funny how she could switch her voice up just like that.

"Hello," she said sounding proper. "Yes. Okay. I can be there in about an hour." She looked at the time on her phone. "Alright, bye."

As soon as she hung up the phone, I was asking questions to see where she had to be at midnight.

"Who was that?"

"My job. One of those hoes called in on a twenty-four-hour case, so I have to go. I'm sorry to cut our night short."

"You were drinking though. You can go to work after that?" I asked, referring to the Long Island she had guzzled down like it was juice and the second one she was sipping on right now.

"Yeah. I'm fine, Grei. All I have to do is sit and chill while they sleep really."

Farah worked as an aide, but she mostly worked nights. Sometimes, she worked during the day, but she told me that was rare.

"Alright. So I guess we're going to be leaving now," I directed toward Knight.

"You can stay, and I can take you home," he offered.

"I don't know," I started, but Farah interrupted me.

"Come on, Grei, don't even. The man said that he could take you home, so don't even try and get out of it. Just 'cause I can't enjoy the rest of my night doesn't mean that you shouldn't either. Here." Pulling out her phone, she swiped it open then pushed a button and snapped a picture of Knight. "I have a picture of him, so if he tries to kidnap or kill you, then we have a record of it, okurrr," she mimicked Cardi.

Laughing, I just shook my head at her as she stood up to leave. I was actually happy that Knight offered to take me home because I wasn't ready to leave. Honestly, I was enjoying my night, and I wanted to get to chill and talk with Knight a bit more. He had seen me at one of my most vulnerable moments, yet he still wasn't judging me.

"Okay. Make sure you text me when you get to work though so I know you got there safe."

"I will. Make sure you text me once Mr. Knight takes you home," she responded with a smirk as she looked at me and Knight.

I didn't know what the smirk meant, but Knight was wearing the same one on his face as if it was contagious. Farah walked out, and it was now just me and Knight. He moved from the seat next to me and sat across from me. His piercing brown eyes were looking directly at me, peering into my soul. My stomach filled with butterflies as the nervousness started to set in, but I was trying not to act like he was affecting me.

"So," I started the conversation, "what do you do?"

We both laughed at me asking the most common, ridiculous question ever. I just didn't know what else to say to break the ice between us because if he stared at me any longer, I was sure that I was going to melt.

"You haven't been out with a real nigga before, have you?"

"I guess not." My eyebrows were pushed together as I answered because I wasn't quite sure how to take what he said.

"You guess not? It's a yes or no question, ma. When somebody asks you a question, always answer it with confidence. Stand by what you're saying, and if you don't know what a person means, then ask them to clarify." He started to drop jewels on me as if we were in school.

"I didn't know it was such a serious question to you. I mean, what do you define a real nigga as?"

"A man that doesn't play games, doesn't go around the bush, and damn sure doesn't play with or put hands on a woman as beautiful as you." Immediately, I started to blush at his comment, even though I felt some type of way that he saw me that way. "A real nigga is me, basically. You don't know me yet, but you'll get to know me."

43

I was speechless. I wasn't used to a man just being so open and blunt with me. Tommy may have been an abusive asshole, but he was a person that rarely came out and said what was on his mind, and dropping jewels? Sometimes I wondered how the hell he was a kingpin because honestly, the nigga never had anything important to say.

This man in front of me though, just from the way he spoke and the way he looked at me intently, I could tell that he was different from Tommy. Just like he wanted to show me the way he could treat me, I wanted to see what he was made of.

"Okay. Show me."

"Oh, I will," he answered while nodding his head with his bottom lip tucked in between his teeth. "You know how to play darts?" He pointed to the dartboard.

"Yeah. You trying to get beat?"

"Ohhhh, you must think you nice?"

"Nah, what you said, mean what I say? I *know* I'm nice," I replied with an emphasis on the word know.

"Aight then." Knight stood from the table. "Let's get another drink and then see who the better man or woman is."

Eyes wide, I spoke, "No, I don't need another drink. I'm already tipsy off this one." I pointed to the glass on the table that was now empty besides the small pieces of ice and lemon wedge that was inside of it.

"Grei, I'm driving, ma. You good to have one more drink," Knight insisted.

Rolling my eyes up into my head, I tilted my head to the side and looked at him.

"Okay, just one more." I was only tipsy, so I was hoping that just one more drink wouldn't send me over the edge.

As we played, we talked shit to each other and got to know more about one another. Well, he actually learned more about me. I mean, I already knew what he did for a living, of course, because he worked for Tommy.

"What's your nationality?" Knight asked as I got prepared to throw a dart.

"What makes you think it's different from yours?" Eyeing the board, I threw the dart, trying to hit a bullseye because right now, Knight was in the lead. I did all that shit talking, so I had to win.

"I remember everything, and I remember that nigga Tommy mentioning some shit before. I just can't recall what it was."

"Nigerian."

"Nice... Is that where you were born?" he asked as I got ready to shoot my second dart.

"Yes, but I don't really remember much from there. We moved here when I was two years old."

Throwing the dart, I hit the bullseye right on the nose.

"Ayyyyeee, I'm catching up to that ass," I boasted with my tongue hanging out.

"You're just catching up a little, but that ain't about shit."

Two hours and a glass of water later, Knight had won twice, and I had won once. It was 2 a.m., and the bar was closing, so we were making our way to the door.

"We have to come back and have a rematch. I wasn't on my A game tonight." I was trying to save face.

"Yeah, okay. You sure looked like you were trying to me." He laughed as he opened the door for me.

I walked ahead of him, but once we were outside, I walked beside him as he led me to his car. He led me to an all-black newer model Malibu. It was nice, but I was surprised that he didn't have some flashy ass car. He may not have been the boss like Tommy, but he was right under him, and I was sure he had money. Like I said though, I didn't care about materialistic things; it was just an observation.

Knight pulled his key from the pockets of his basketball shorts and hit the button on the remote to unlock the doors. Walking around to my side, he opened the door for me and allowed me to get in. Tommy always opened the doors for me, but this was different because Knight was giving me butterflies in my stomach while Tommy made me feel like I needed to throw up. Sliding into the car, I sat on the black leather seats.

It wasn't the Rolls Royce or the Audi that I was used to, but his car was nice as hell. The dashboard was fully loaded. Knight got into the car and started the engine using push to start. The air immediately started to blast through the vents, but he turned it off and rolled our windows down. The night air was feeling great, so the AC wasn't even needed. I loved the summer for that very reason. Once it was night time, that breeze was everything.

Knight connected his iPhone to the radio, and music blared through the speakers. Looking at the dashboard, it said that the song playing was Nas's song K-I-S-S-I-N-G.

Picture us married, you and me; K-I-S-S-I-N-G
I remember the first time, girl you and me; F-U-C-K-I-N-G
Girl picture us married, you and me; K-I-S-S-I-N-G
I remember the first time, girl you and me; F-U-C-K-I-N-G

He sang along with the lyrics as he gripped my thigh through my jeans. I didn't know if it was the way he was touching me or the way Nas rapped where you could see everything that he was saying, but I could picture me and Knight walking down the aisle and living happily. How could I even be seeing such a thing when this wasn't my man but his friend and worker? How could I be seeing a future with a man that I barely even knew?

I wasn't one of those women that fell in love with any man that I had a conversation with or started to picture us together after just meeting. That wasn't my M.O. at all, so this was a weird ass feeling for me. Trying to shift my thoughts, I looked out of the window and realized that we were going in the total opposite direction of Farah's house. Matter of fact, he hadn't even asked me where she lived.

Reaching over, I turned the radio down.

"Where are we going?"

"I gotta make a stop real quick, then I can take you to ya cuz house. If you want," he added.

"A stop where?" I was not trying to be that ride or die chick in the passenger seat while he drove to serve fiends or no shit like that. Sorry, but I wasn't trying to be caught up in anything.

"To grab some food," he said nonchalantly, and I felt a bit of relief. I didn't want to end our night early, but I would have if he was going to do anything like that.

About fifteen minutes later, we pulled up to a pizza spot called Luciano's. I had heard of the place and passed by it before, but never went in. Knight pulled up right in front and cut the engine.

"Hold up." Getting out of the car, I watched him as he walked around to my side and opened the door for me. Even though Tommy opened the car door for me, it was different. He just did it out of habit, but Knight was doing it because he wanted to. Maybe it was just because I was actually interested in him that the gesture meant more.

Getting out of the car, Knight led the way into the pizza shop. It was pretty dead since it was late at night. Most pizzerias were closed at this time, so they were probably about to close. There were about four tables with four chairs at each table around the red, black, and white decorated pizza shop.

"My man, Knight," the man behind the counter spoke with a bright smile on his face. You could tell he was an Italian because he just had the aura about him. He was a round man, with a large belly and average sized legs. He was about five-seven and had jet black hair.

"What's up, Lou?" Knight said as they shook hands.

"Who's this pretty young lady you have with you?"

"Grei, this is Lou. Lou, this is my future wife, Grei." Knight looked back at me and winked his left eye.

My stomach started to flutter at just a wink. He had me feeling all types of emotions about him. Lou came from behind the counter and walked over to me.

"It's nice to meet you, Grei. You are a sight for sore eyes, aren't you? Listen here." He moved in close and whispered in my ear, "If Knight messes up, I'm always available." He let out a hearty laugh afterward.

I knew he was just joking, but it was still a little weird that a man my father's age was even saying something like that. Maybe because Nigerian men would never say anything like that.

"Lou, don't be whispering in my lady's ear, man. I'd hate to fuck ya old ass up," Knight said with a light laugh.

He threw his hands up in surrender. "I'm just trying to let the young lady know that she has options," he said with a laugh, and his stomach jiggled.

"Yeah, aight. Grei, you want something?" I would say no, but I was actually hungry. The liquor had kicked in, and I felt like I had a case of the munchies now.

"Yeah, a slice of cheese pizza and a five-piece mild wings."

"And what you want, boss?" Lou asked Knight.

"Two slices of pepperoni pizza with garlic parm wings."

"Okay, coming right up. You know what?" Lou stopped like he had just had the perfect idea. "Knight, why don't you come back so I can show you the new oven I got, man."

"Aight, cool." Walking to the front door, he locked it then turned back around toward me. "You okay with sitting out here for a minute while I check this shit out? I don't really care to see it, but Lou a cool ass old head, so I'mma check it out for that nigga."

"Okay. I'm good with sitting out here." I smiled at him.

"Damn, ya smile beautiful as fuck."

There it was; my stomach was fluttering yet again. Knight turned around and walked back toward the kitchen and through the large metal doors. Sitting down at the table in the far right, I sat so that I could see the door and also the rest of the room around me. It wasn't that I was paranoid, but I loved being able to see a whole room.

Pulling my phone out, I sent Farah a message, letting her know that I was still with Knight and didn't know what time I was going home. I didn't want her to be at work wondering if I was okay. Just as I was about to lock my phone, it started to vibrate in my hands. The small hairs on my arms stood up from looking at the name that was displaying on the screen.

Tommy's name was displayed across the screen. I didn't know

whether I should answer or let it go to voicemail. *Fuck it,* I thought, as I accepted the call and answered it.

"H-hello." Taking a deep breath, I tried to calm my nerves down.

"Where the fuck is yo' ass at!" he yelled through the phone. I pushed the button on the side, turning it down like I wasn't the only person in the room.

"Huh?" I asked, trying to stall.

"If you can huh, you can fucking hear! Where are you, huh, bitch? I get back to my house thinking that I'm going to be seeing my bitch, and you not fucking here. Where are you?"

"I just went to grab something to eat," I lied.

A sinister laugh came from the other end of the phone that sent chills through my spine.

"I already saw that you took a bunch of shit. What, you call yaself moving out? If you're not back within twenty-four hours and I have to come looking for you, I'm kicking your ass. You can never leave me."

Click!

I looked at my phone, and he had hung up on me.

"You good?" Knight asked as he walked in the room and started walking toward me.

Looking down at myself, I realized that my chest was heaving up and down. I was breathing like I had just run a 5k. I tried to normalize my breathing without him noticing it.

"Ummm, yeah. I'm fine," I answered, flashing him a small smile.

He gave me an uneasy look then did a 360 around the pizza shop like he was making sure there was nobody in there, even though he had locked the door himself. I hoped he didn't think I was trying to set him up or no shit like that.

"'Iight," he finally responded. "Our food should be done in a minute."

"That quick?"

"Hell yeah. That oven he got some crazy big shit." Knight sat at the table across from me.

"So, what's your dreams and aspirations; ya know, shit like that?"

A smile instantly spread across my Hershey toned face. Maybe he had never dated before, but that was not the way you were supposed to ask that question. It was still cute though.

"Well, my dreams and aspirations and shit like that is to be a writer. Ever since I was a little girl, I loved writing, and that was always my favorite subject in school."

"Word? That's cool as shit. So what's stopping you?"

With my head tilted to the side, I thought about his question. It was so crazy that this simple question had never been asked to me by anyone ever, not even Tommy.

"I'm scared to fail... nervous to let the inside world in on my thoughts. What if I think I'm good, and it's terrible? Then, I never really had anyone encouraging me to go after my dreams, ya know. Also, a lot of people think writing is just a side thing to do, but I want it to be my way of life and means of income."

"You can't be afraid to go after what you want. You damn sure can't be thinking about failing before you even try it. You're saying what if it's terrible, but what if it's great?"

Nodding my head, I agreed with him. "You're right. Maybe I'll start writing and see where it takes me." What did I have to lose? In my eyes, being with Tommy was the worst, so it could only go up from here, right?

"Anyway, what are your dreams and aspirations and shit?" I asked, mocking him as we both laughed.

"Well, being a boss," he said, opening his arms wide like the whole world was his. "I never saw me working for anyone. I never saw myself being a corporate nigga. All I knew was that I didn't want to work for anyone, and I wanted to be rich."

"But you work for Tommy, so technically, that's not the same as being your own boss," I pointed out and immediately regretted letting the words spill from my mouth.

Laughing, he licked his succulent lips and looked at me with an amused look on his face.

"Is that what he told you? I mean, I know that's what it looks like, but did he actually ever tell you that I worked for him?" He put his hand to his chest to emphasize 'I'.

Thinking back, I checked my mental rolodex. He had never actually said that that I could mention, but he was always referring to himself as a boss.

"Well, not really, but he always refers to himself as a boss. I mean, you can't both be the boss, or are you?" I asked with my eyebrows raised.

"Pizza and wings are ready." Lou came from the back with two bags in his hand. One held the pizza and one held the wings.

Knight didn't hesitate to get up without answering my question, and I wished that Lou had just waited five more minutes. He grabbed the bags from Lou's hand and slapped him up.

"Aight, man."

"Alright," Lou responded as they fist bumped.

"It was nice meeting you," I said as I went to give Lou a handshake.

"I'm Italian; we hug," he said with his arms wide and belly sticking out, waiting for a hug.

"Nahhh, Lou; you trying to get fucked up. You better take that damn handshake. Matter of fact, you ain't even getting that. Come on, Grei." I didn't know he was serious until he started walking to the door.

"Umm, bye," I shot back at Lou as I walked out the door that Knight was now holding open for me.

Once we got outside, Knight opened the back door and put the food on the floor then opened the door for me.

"Do you want to go to ya cousin's or my crib?" he asked as soon as he got into the driver's seat and started the car. Knight looked over at me, I'm assuming waiting for my response before he started driving in any direction.

"Honestly, I really don't want our night to end, but I also don't want to go to your house and you think that means we're having sex." However he responded to this was going to let me know how I should deal with him from this moment on. If he was pressed for sex and thought that I was going to be fucking him on the first night, then he wasn't for me.

"I'm not going to pressure you to do anything you don't want to do. I'm not that type of nigga." *Perfect*, I thought.

"Okay, then we can go to your house."

"Iight, cool."

KNIGHT

*G*rei was chill and cool like I already thought she would be. You could tell she had a head on her shoulders, and she wasn't anything like this ditzy Dora hoes that be out here. Looking over at the passenger seat, she was looking out at the streets like she was in a new town and hadn't been here before. I could tell that she had a lot of shit on her mind. It was probably that fuck ass nigga Tommy.

I was surprised when I got to the bar and saw that she was there and wasn't with that nigga. I didn't even ask her about the nigga because I couldn't really care less about his ass. His bitch was about to be mine, so if he was smart, he was out finding him a new one. Pulling into my building garage, I found my designated space and backed in.

Cutting the engine, I got out to open the door for Grei and to get the food from the back. I wasn't an opening the doors ass nigga, but for her, I was doing it. She wasn't like those other bitches I just knocked off and sent they asses home. We walked side by side as I led the way through the lobby and to the elevators.

"This is nice," she commented on a painting that was on the wall. It was of a black man and a woman that was pregnant. The owner of the building was black, so there were pictures of black families, men, and women all over the building.

"Yeah. It's nice ass pictures all around this shit on every floor."

"That's different."

Ding!

The elevator doors opened for us to get in. Letting her in first, I got in and stood beside her. Pushing the button for my floor, the doors closed. We were silent in the elevator as we rode it. I didn't know if she was nervous or what, but she was as quiet as a church mouse like she was sitting in a library.

Ding!

The elevator went off again, ending the awkward silence. Again, I let her get out first and followed behind before I walked beside her. Stopping at my door, I put my hand up and let it read my print.

Beep!

The door opened, and I hit the one light switch that would turn on all the other lights.

"Oh my God," Grei said as she looked around. "This is nice as hell. I'm sorry, but when you think of an apartment in a building, you think of a small cramped place, and trust me, I don't mind; it's better than what I have. This is just nice as fuck." Her eyes were wide open as she spoke, and I couldn't help but laugh.

"It's a condo, so it's a lot more space. Shit, I just don't have a house because it's only me, so ain't no point." Closing the door behind us, I took my shoes off then headed to the dining room area to put the food bags down on the table.

"How long have you lived here?"

"Uhhh, about a year now," I answered, taking a minute to think back.

"This is really nice, Knight. It's a dope layout and all."

"Thanks, ma, but I ain't bring you over here to be drooling all over my shit," I joked.

"Ha, ha, ha. I'm not drooling at all, just giving your ugly ass a compliment."

"Oh, and now I'm ugly, huh? Damn, a nigga sure thought he was fine the way ya pussy damn near creamed in the club for me that night," I said, referring to my birthday night. She ain't have to admit to shit because the way she stared me down had told me all that I needed to know. I already knew shorty was feeling me, even if she tried to play hard to get.

Her sexy, slanted eyes were looking straight at me. They were a little bigger than usual, like she was in shock that I knew how much she was feeling me. They went back to their regular size, and she walked over to me before she spoke.

"I liked what I saw just as much as you liked what you saw."

Her face was inches from mine now. Grei was really beautiful as fuck. Her body was crazy with the fat ass and small waist. Her waist wasn't like those Instagram models either; she had a little stomach, just nothing crazy, and it was sexy as fuck. I didn't like when bitches were walking around with abs or stomachs so small their body looked disproportionate.

Grei's Hershey skin tone was crazy as hell too. When they say melanin dipped in gold, she looked like her shit was really dipped in gold. Her skin was perfect with not a blemish in sight. And those thick ass thighs would definitely get a nigga every time. She was just sexy as hell. Walking closer to her, I put my arm around her waist. Her body didn't tense up a bit.

"You right. So we might as well skip the dates and all that and just be together then, huh?"

My dick was up against her, and I knew she could feel it because the shit I was working with was hard to miss.

"Nah, you're not getting this for cheap or easy. You're going to wine and dine me first, then maybe we can be together." Grei pulled my arms from around her waist and stepped back.

"Let's eat now. You still going to turn Netflix on?" she asked like nothing had just happened between us.

Laughing, I responded, "Yeah. Let me turn that on for you since we dating and all."

I knew she was trying to play hard to get, but I didn't care. If she had let me hit tonight, I wouldn't have looked at her like a hoe because

I knew she wasn't that type of person. I knew everything that happened in these streets and would have known if she had a name for herself. She didn't though, because that nigga Tommy kept her locked up.

I respected her for demanding what she deserved though, and a nigga had no problem wining and dining her. The shit wouldn't stop even when we got together.

FARAH

lick, click, click
    My heels tapped against the concrete as I made my way to the private plane that was waiting for me. Since leaving the bar, I had stopped at home to change my outfit and was now wearing a cherry red trench coat with nothing but a matching lace thong and bra on underneath. Nobody knew what my true occupation was, and I wasn't planning on letting anyone know any time soon. I knew what people would think and how people would look at me if they knew the truth, and I wasn't ready to be scrutinized.

Growing up, I had to be on pins and needles. Do this, don't do that, wear this, don't wear that. It never stopped. When I finally was old enough and got my money up enough to move out of my parents' house, things changed. Now, I wouldn't act like I loved my job, but I didn't necessarily hate it either. It was just like any other job that had its pros and cons.

Reaching the plane, the door was already open, and there was a man outside of it dressed in a black suit and a black hat. His arms were crossed in front of him, and when I walked up, he greeted me with a head nod. He didn't say anything as he held his hand out and helped me onto the plane. I walked in, and there he was.

He was sitting with one of his legs crossed over the other, and smoking on a cigar. I already knew that it was one of Cuban's finest because that was all that he smoked.

"Farah. Hello, sweetheart." He stood up and greeted me with a hug and kiss on the cheek. He was dressed dapper in a navy-blue suit with a black shirt and no tie. On his feet were a pair of black dress shoes, and his beard and hair were lined up perfectly as it always was. This man was always dressed nicely, and he always looked his best.

It didn't matter that this was work. He always made me feel comfortable, and I always felt like we were old friends or really in a relationship.

"Hello, Mr. Doug," I responded, calling him by his first name. He reached out for my hand and kissed the back of it. This was one of my easiest jobs because he always made it enjoyable. His manners, his chill demeanor, and his laid-back attitude was so attractive, and he was pretty easy on the eyes.

Doug stood about six feet two. He had calm blue eyes, and his skin wasn't pale; it had an olive tone to it. His hair was always freshly cut, and I'd never seen him wearing the same suit twice. He was Italian, and I wasn't exactly sure what his profession was, but that was none of my business.

"I have to go to New York for some business. I know that you love the city, so I figured why not pleasure and business. You up for it?" he asked me as he looked at me with this bright smile on my face.

"Of course," I answered with a smile matching his.

"Luke!" he called out to the man that helped me inside the private plane. He stuck his head in the door. "We are ready." The man nodded his head.

"You." Doug looked at me. "Go in the back and get in my favorite position."

My insides melted. Not only was Dough charismatic, the sex with him was bomb, and I always looked forward to it. No words were exchanged as I dropped my trench coat and walked to the room in the back of the plane. I didn't need to look back. I knew that he was right behind me because he was squeezing my ass as I entered the room.

GREI

"Good morning," the Uber driver greeted me as I got into the back seat of their car.

"Good morning," I responded and closed the door. As soon as the door was closed, he pulled into the morning traffic, going toward Farah's house.

Looking out the window, a smile that I wasn't even trying to display spread across my face. Last night was one of the best nights that I'd had in a long time. Knight was cool as hell, and there were stories about him that I'd heard, but it seemed like none of that shit was true. He really just seemed like a laid-back dude, and he was easy to get along with. I mean, you could tell that he was confident as hell in the way he carried himself.

Last night, we ate, watched TV, and just laughed all night. He smoked, and I sipped a little wine while we chilled. There was just a really chill vibe between us like we had been friends forever. When he asked if we could be together, only the Lord knew how I wanted to scream out yes, but I knew that I needed to get my life in order before jumping into anything with anyone. It felt good to chill with him, but I wanted us to take things slowly. I did things fast with Tommy, and you see how that shit ended.

Buzz!

My phone vibrated in my hand. Looking at it, it was an unknown number. *Must be Tommy's ass,* I thought as I ignored it. He had called me two more times last night, making sure I knew how many hours I had left until I needed to be back at the house. He could just leave voicemails like he did last night.

I was surprised to see so many cars out since it was six in the morning. I knew people had to go to work, but I thought that most people went around eight. Still thinking about last night, I wondered what Knight was going to think when he woke up and saw me gone. I hope he didn't think it meant I didn't want to fuck with him, but I didn't want to be waking up to a man in the morning that wasn't my nigga.

Ten minutes later, we pulled up to Farah's house. Her complex was still quiet since it was so early in the morning. The Uber driver pulled in front of the address.

"Thank you," I said as I opened the door and got out.

Walking up to the door, I felt the pockets of my jeans, searching for the key. Farah had given it to me before leaving the bar yesterday. I didn't feel it in the front left pocket where I knew I put it, so I started patting the other pockets, trying to find just where I put it.

"Damn, where did I—" I started, but when I looked up, my voice got caught in my chest.

There was Tommy, pulling up in his truck. I didn't know if he had perfect timing or had been watching the house all night, but what I did know was that I better get my ass in the house or end up dead. Frantically, I started to check my pockets and then started to dig in my purse. I needed to find these keys like I needed my next breath.

I didn't see the damn key anywhere, and I knew it had to have fallen out somewhere. My phone started to vibrate in my hand. Looking at it again, it was the same unknown number that called me before. Looking up, Tommy was walking toward me, and he wasn't on the phone, so it couldn't be him calling.

"Hello," I answered the call quickly.

"Yo, so you just dip on a nigga like that? Shit, I don't think you stole anything, so you didn't have to leave like a damn thief in the night, Grei," Knight's voice came through the phone.

As he spoke into my ear, Tommy stood in my face. His light, usually even-toned skin was now red; even the tips of his ears were red. He looked a mess in a black wife beater that was torn and a pair of black trunks. Why he even had trunks on, I didn't fucking know, but he did.

"Hello?" Knight said into the phone.

"Get in the car," was all Tommy said.

Pulling the phone from my ear, I disconnected the call and held it down by my side. I didn't even want Knight to hear the heated exchange between us.

"No. I'm done; this is over." I refused to not hold my own because I was fed up. He could just let me go and be with one of those bitches he was messing with.

"This isn't over until I say it's over. You think you can just leave me? That's what you think?" His face was twisted, and his nostrils were flaring.

"Tommy, just let me go. You have bitches you can be with. Why can't you just leave me alone?" I started to cry. I just wanted to be free of him. His control, his torture, his anger, anything that was attached to him; I just wanted to be free.

"I told you when we got together that this was forever, and I meant that."

Grabbing me by the neck, he applied pressure and pulled, almost dragged me to his truck. Tommy pulled open the door with so much force that it flew open. He looked like The Hulk as he breathed hard, and sweat started to pour down his face. His left hand was still on my neck as he pushed me into his car and into the passenger seat, slamming the door behind me.

Tears were freely flowing down my face. Tommy started to walk around the front of the car, and I looked at the door handle, thinking if I should make a run for it or not. Where would I run to though? Fuck that. If anything was going to happen to me, then I'd rather for me to be fighting than to not try at all.

As soon as he was opening the driver's side door, I pulled on my door handle and pushed. Nothing. It didn't budge. *Fuckkkk!* I wanted to scream out, but only said it in my head. This damn door had been getting stuck for weeks now, and Tommy kept saying he was going to get it fixed. It looked like it was actually working in his damn favor.

Getting into the driver's seat, the car was already on, and Tommy pulled the gear into drive and pulled off. The almost forty-minute drive home was quiet, and I was on edge the entire way. He was too quiet, and I knew that meant nothing good. Tommy always showed his rage, and the fact that he was quiet as a mouse was scaring me. If this door had opened, I would have been jumped out and hauled ass because, at this point, I was afraid that I was fighting for my life.

Finally, we pulled up to the house, and my heart started to beat faster the closer we got to the gate. Then it beat even faster when he pulled into the driveway and parked. The engine stopped, and it felt like my breathing was now trapped in my chest, unable to exhale. Scared to exhale. I was afraid to make a sound because maybe if I didn't, then he would forget all that I had done and just how pissed at me he was.

Tommy got out of the car, closed his door behind him, then walked over to the passenger seat to let me out. My seat belt was on because of the beeping noise his truck would do unless it was on, and I didn't want anything to agitate him even more. Basically, I was trying to get in and find a way out of this house again without a hand laid on me. Taking my seat belt off, I got out of the car and walked toward the door with Tommy hot on my trail.

We reached the door, and I opened it without a key. This mansion was built like Fort Knox, and since people couldn't even get past the gate, we rarely locked the door. Walking in, everything looked the same, but it felt so different. The door closed behind me, and the real Tommy turned on.

I felt his hands grab my hair yet again as he pulled, and my neck jerked back. I even heard my shit crack from him yanking so hard. My long bundles were wrapped in his fist.

"You're leaving me! After everything I did for your ungrateful ass."

He pulled harder, and the tears I was trying to hold started to pour out. This sew-in was on tight, and it felt like my hair was being pulled from my scalp.

Tommy used all the strength he had and pulled me up the stairs. It hurt like hell as my ass hit every damn stair on the way up.

"Get off me!" I yelled. I said that I was tired of not sticking up for myself, and I meant that shit. "Let my hair go!"

"Ohhh yeah, you feeling yaself, huh? Must be whatever nigga was in that pussy last night or better yet this morning. Where the fuck were you coming from?"

Finally, we reached the top of the stairs, and he pulled me into the room. He let my hair go and ripped the rest of his shirt off and stood back with his arms opened wide.

"Get up. Come on. Fight me with ya tough ass, Grei. Come on."

I couldn't believe this. I had never seen this nigga fight anybody. He ran a whole fucking drug empire, and this was the first time I ever saw him in a dispute with anyone. For him to be trying to fight me was really fucking pathetic. I now knew that he was truly a fucking coward.

Everything in me wanted to get up and fight him, but no matter how much I knew how to fight, this was a man, and I wasn't dumb. The way he was pulling my hair, he would do anything to beat my ass, and those size twelve feet was the last thing I wanted to be stomping me out like a bitch in the street. Putting my head down, I shook it back and forth because I was disgusted and in disbelief.

"That's what the fuck I thought. You not so fucking tough." Leaning down, he got in my face. Grabbing my chin, he picked it up so that my wet eyes were looking right into his red ones.

"If you ever try to leave me again, I'm going to kill you. If I ever have to come get you, I'm going to kill you. I'm the only nigga for you. Now go soak in the tub because you smell like you been laid up all fucking night; and if I even find out that's true, I'll kill you." Pushing my chin with so much force that my head nearly spun, he stood up and walked off. How the fuck was I going to get out of here now?

KNIGHT

Sitting outside of Monroe County jail, I waited for them to free my nigga Cruz up out them gates. He had only been in there for a couple months, so it was nothing, but I still needed my nigga out here with me. Cruz was a nigga that I had grown up with, and together, we were the real masterminds behind this drug shit. We really owned the streets while we let that nigga Tommy play the forefront.

Looking at the time, I shook my head because I knew this nigga was supposed to be out almost an hour ago. I pulled out the small jar of cranberry kush I had and started to roll up. Yeah, there were cops all around this muthafucka, but there was more shit going on in the damn world other than me getting high on their premises.

This nigga Cruz was in jail for some dumb ass shit. He was a crazy ass nigga, but he could never hold shit in. He didn't know the time and place to let his crazy out. I was crazy, but my shit was different. Yeah, I knew there were times you just couldn't control the shit, but he never could, and his anger was what landed him doing a couple of months in this shitty ass place.

Just as I licked the blunt closed, I looked up and watched as Cruz walked toward my car with a smile on his face. This nigga was smiling like he had just come from a five-star resort. He was wearing a white wife beater and a pair of black jeans; must have been what the nigga had on when he went in.

"What's up, man?" I slapped him up as he opened the passenger door and got in. "Fuck you so happy for?"

"Shit, 'cause I'm out of that muthafucka. I don't know why we can't just pay 12 to stay out of that muthafucka."

"'Cause I'm not paying no fucking pigs for protection." I was against that shit. I wasn't about to pay they asses to protect shit. Why the fuck should they get any of my hard-earned money?

"Man, we need them muthafuckas in our pocket," Cruz started to explain as I pulled off. "Just think, we would have insight on what's going on, protection—man, that shit would be a good move."

"I don't know, man." I wasn't saying it was a bad idea at all. I mean, the shit did have its benefits. We would be able to get inside information, and we wouldn't be doing no dumb ass jail time behind bullshit, but I was hesitant as fuck to start paying 12.

"Yeah, yeah. So what's been up?" Cruz asked, putting his seat back, and I started to fill him in on everything that had been going on. Our spots were doing good for the most part, but there were a couple problems that needed to be handled.

"This nigga fucking up. It's pretty much time to delete this nigga because having him around is defeating the fucking purpose," I explained to Cruz as we sped through traffic.

We were smoking on our second blunt filled with Cali's finest. Like I said, I always watched what went down at my spots so I knew when anything was going wrong. Niggas were stealing right under Tommy's coke filled nose, and he didn't know a thing about it. Now I was on my way to deal with it.

Having him as the "person in charge" while I played the enforcer was really defeating the purpose when it came to dealing with these niggas. It all seemed like a good idea though because I didn't want a target on my back. I didn't want cops recognizing me and trying to pull me over for every little thing. They knew of me, maybe saw me, but shit, I was a minion compared to Tommy, and that's how I needed it to be. That might have to change though because I didn't like my money being jeopardized.

I pulled up right in front of the red trap house on Grand Avenue. There were a couple of niggas shooting dice on the porch, and I already knew that more than one nigga was dying today. Shaking my head, I cut the engine and pulled my Glock 19 from under the seat. Cruz went under his seat and grabbed the Glock 40. We didn't have to exchange any words, because he already knew where my shit was in the car.

My shit was already loaded, so there wasn't a need to check. Opening the door, Cruz followed my lead as we walked to the porch. I was dressed the part, dressed in all black as I walked calmly to the porch. As soon as niggas saw us walking up, they started to straighten up. I may have not been the boss to them, but I was the enforcer, and they already knew how a nigga gave it up.

"Yo, what's up, Knight?" Dallas greeted me but also basically alerted niggas to straighten up. They started to stand straight up and tried to swiftly pick the dice up like I hadn't already spotted them niggas shooting dice.

"Don't 'what's up' me, man. Why y'all niggas out here shooting dice, making it hot and shit? If the cops roll past, they got a reason to stop here."

"My bad, Knight." Dallas continued to speak for the group. "It's the end of the month, so you know, it's just slow as hell. Man, them crackers ain't gon' fuck with us for shooting a little dice."

Chuckling, I shook my head at this dumb ass nigga. Dallas was the head of this trap house, so I guess he felt it was his job to speak for up for the house, which it was. If this trap failed or came up short, it was his ass. His future was already written for him, so the fact that he was trying to speak up about anything was funny as hell to me.

"Dallas, let me speak to you for a minute, man." I brushed past him and walked into the house. He followed me inside, and Cruz walked in behind him.

The house was set up like people actually lived here, even though that wasn't the case. There was a love seat, a couch, and a recliner in the living room, with a 40-inch television on a black stand. The black coffee table in the middle was littered with to-go containers and garbage all over it.

"Knight, I swear, man. I'm on my P's and Q's when it comes to this shit, man. Ain't shit going to go down, yo."

I looked at this mark ass nigga with my hands crossed in front of me. This nigga hadn't been a leader to begin with, but again, I was giving that nigga Tommy the benefit of the doubt. Dallas was Tommy's younger brother, and that was really the only reason his ass got this job. Tommy vouched for him, so I decided to give him a chance. I didn't know this nigga was going to be such a fuck up.

"So, you're telling me you got shit handled around here?" I questioned, waiting for the lie that I knew was coming straight to my face.

"Yeah, man. I got everything handled," he said as a confident smile spread across his face. This nigga must have thought I was really going to believe the shit he was giving me.

"Okay. So you have everything handled?" I repeated.

I felt the vein in the left side of my temple twitch. It was so hard hiding my anger that my shit was literally getting ready to bust. There were two things that I hated, and that was a liar and a thief. This nigga was both as he lied straight to my face without so much as a drop of sweat falling to indicate that he was lying.

In one swift motion, I grabbed my gun from my hip and pulled it on the nigga. At first, I was planning on talking to the nigga first. There was no way I was letting him live, but I thought that he just might tell the truth instead of ignoring me, and maybe I could hear the nigga out. Maybe he had a sick relative or some bullshit, but at least he would try to redeem himself. This nigga was, instead, lying to my face like it was nothing, and I couldn't even hesitate to kill his ass now.

Pop, pop!

I shot him two times in the head, and his body instantly dropped like a bag of potatoes.

"Damn. I knew you was gonna do that shit." Cruz shook his head as he looked at Dallas's corpse. "That nigga did two of the things you hated the most, bruh." He chuckled.

I didn't say anything as I walked to the back of the house to the wooden door. Opening the door, there stood Trell filled with a room of naked bitches. Trell was a nigga that worked at this house, and he had the most potential. He was in here making sure the work got bagged and bitches didn't steal.

"Yo, come out here for a second." I stepped out the door, and Trell did as well, but he didn't fully turn his back to the bitches that were in the back room. "I been watching you, my nigga, and you show a lot of potential. More than anybody that works in this bitch, and especially that stupid ass nigga Dallas." I pointed to his dead body with brains splattered all over the couch he was standing by. Trell didn't flex as he looked over at his lifeless body then back over to me.

"You in charge of this shit now. I'mma call the cleanup crew for that nigga."

"Nah, you ain't gotta do that. Those niggas that was out there playing dice and shit instead of working gon' do it. It's time for me to really show these niggas that I ain't shit to play with," Trell said with a serious look on his face.

"Shit, say no more." I slapped him up and walked toward the door. Walking past Dallas, I wanted to spit on him, but I didn't just in case these niggas didn't really know how to get rid of a body properly. "Fuck nigga," I spoke as I walked out the door with Cruz behind me. The niggas on the porch were quiet as church mice, sounding like they weren't even breathing as we walked off and got in the car.

After dropping Cruz off at his crib, I drove in silence as I headed home. Cruz and I became friends while we were in the womb because our mothers were best friends. He was basically like my brother, and he always had my back. Our mothers were both single mothers and decided to raise us under the same roof. I didn't know if it was for support, or if it was just cost-efficient.

I had never met my father, and my mother never really talked about him much. Sometimes, when she was talking to Cruz's mother, she would say things like he was no good, or he wasn't shit. I didn't know a name, a race, nothing. All I knew was that he wasn't in my life, and in return, my mother raised me until the streets did.

We grew up in St. Simons projects in a four-bedroom apartment. Both of our mothers worked their asses off as CNA's. When we were younger, they would work in shifts. One would work a day shift while the other worked the night shift so that one of them could be there to take care of us at all times. Then we grew up and shit changed.

They had to provide for us, bills got higher, and it became almost impossible for them to work in shifts and take care of us as well. We were fourteen-year-old boys with no male guidance and limited parental supervision, so it was nothing for us to be out all hours of the night. It was nothing for us to smoke our first blunt or get drunk for the first time at fourteen. By the time we hit sixteen though, we were tired and fed up with seeing our mothers struggle without any help, so we got to it.

Pulling into the parking garage to my condo, I parked in my designated spot. I wasn't ready to go in the house, and I knew just exactly what a nigga needed. Picking up my phone from the cup holder, I unlocked it with my fingerprint and called up Finesse, then I put the phone on speaker. Finesse was a chick that I had been messing with for a couple of months now.

She was a cool chick, but sometimes, she acted like we had something more than what we had. I told her from the jump that our relationship would be strictly casual and nothing more. That was good, and everything worked out great for a couple of weeks, and then it started. She wanted me to spend the night or take her out, and I wasn't with none of that shit.

"Hello," she answered the phone.

"Yo, what's up?"

"Nothing, Knight. Just getting ready to go to this cookout my people having. Why, what's up?" There was eagerness in her voice, even though she was trying to hide it.

"Shit, I was gon' ride through real quick, but if you going to ya people's shit, then I can hit you another time."

"No!" she practically yelled through the phone, and I looked at the

69

phone with narrow eyes. "You can come through now. I'm not leaving for a minute anyway."

Now I knew why her ass had yelled in the phone like that. She needed daddy's dick, and her ass was willing to stay home the rest of the day if it meant I was coming through.

"Aight."

Hanging up the phone, I opened the arm rest and pulled out the already rolled blunt. I hated rolling every time I wanted to smoke, so I would always roll a couple at one time. Lighting it, I inhaled the smoke and pulled out of the parking lot.

Within twenty minutes, I was pulling up to Finesse's crib. She lived close by, but I had to stop at the store and get rubbers. I never fucked any bitch raw because I wasn't trying to have kids with a bunch of random women. Pulling up in front of Finesse's house, I parked on the street and pulled my phone out before I dialed her number.

"Yes?"

"Open the door." Again, I hung up the phone without waiting for a response.

My engine was still running as I waited for her to come open the door. It wasn't that I was scared or anything like that. She lived in a fucked-up neighborhood, but it had nothing to do with that. I wasn't about to be on no porch waiting for a bitch to open the door, and if she took too long, then I was pulling off.

In less than a minute, the door was opening, and I could see the light shining from inside. Finally, turning my engine off, I got out of my car and hit the button on my remote to lock the doors. Nobody fucked with my shit; it was just out of habit. Reaching her front door, Finesse stood back with the door wide open, and when I walked in, she closed it behind me.

Looking her up and down, I licked my lips. Finesse may have been annoying as shit sometimes, but the way she looked made up for all of that. That was the only reason I kept fucking with her. Finesse was beautiful. She was a brown-skinned chick with a slim thick body, and this shit was all knife; it was not from her momma. The whole hood knew that she had paid for this body, and she didn't give a fuck that they did.

Her body was like Bernice Burgos, and she was pretty in the face. She was wearing one of those lace front wigs with a part in the middle. Finesse was wearing a pair of short, tight ass Calvin Klein shorts and a matching sports bra, leaving little to the imagination. Her pussy print was showing through her shorts.

"Long time no see," Finesse said as she looked me up and down. Her legs were crossed as she spoke.

"What you mean? You just saw me last week." My brows furrowed.

"Yeaaah, but that's a long time, Knight. You know I need some of that every day." She bit her bottom lip as she looked at my dick through my pants.

"Well shit, what we sitting here talking for then? Come take this shit."

That was all I had to say, and Finesse was on her knees. Finesse unbuckled my belt with no problem and pulled my pants down. Pulling my briefs down, Finesse pulled out my semi-erect dick. Jacking it with her right hand, she licked the tip a couple of times with her pierced tongue.

My dick was now standing at attention, and she wasted no time devouring it in her mouth. Finesse gave the best head, and she had no trouble getting all ten inches inside of her mouth and down her throat. My hand was on the back of her head as she ate my dick up like it was her favorite meal.

"Fuckkkk," I said through gritted teeth as I leaned against the wall. Moaning wasn't my thing, and I wasn't about to start now. A nigga might yell out a lil' bit but moaning just wasn't in me.

My dick was getting wetter as she bobbed up and down on my dick. Her spit was making it wetter as she gagged, and I could feel the back of her throat touching the tip. She always gave bomb ass head like she hadn't sucked my dick in months. Finesse had both hands on my dick, twisting them around it while she sucked it.

Buzz, buzz

Looking at my phone in my hand, it was Grei. I hadn't heard from her since she hung up on me earlier today.

"Hold up, ma." I patted Finesse's head so she could let up. Catching my breath, I answered the phone.

"Yo?"

"Knight, pl-please come get me," I heard a terrified Grei from the other end of the line. She was whispering into the phone.

"What? Where you at? What's going on?" Stepping back from Finesse, I pulled up my boxers and pants in one swipe.

"I'm at Tommy's house, and he…" Her voice faded out. "Please, just come get me, please."

"I'm on my way, aight? I'm on my way!" I yelled in the phone as I opened the door and bounced. I didn't say shit to Finesse as she stood there looking stuck with saliva still around her mouth and dick on her breath.

GREI

*A*s soon as Tommy fell asleep, I crept out of bed and grabbed my phone from the dresser drawer that he had put it in. After beating my ass, he made me take a bath then fucked me until he fell asleep. I didn't want to have sex, but I also didn't want to resist because there was no telling what he would do. Here I was, crouched in a corner in our walk-in closet. It was big enough that I had room, but I still felt anxiety because I was so scared of Tommy waking up and realizing that I wasn't by his side.

The first person I called was Farah, but she didn't answer, so I had no choice but to call Knight. He had given me his number last night when we were drinking, but I had saved it as a note and not a contact. That was how damn drunk I was. I knew I probably sounded crazy as hell on the phone, but I felt a bit of relief when he told me that he was on his way.

Sitting in the closet, I counted down the minutes as I waited for Knight to come and rescue me. I couldn't believe that the man that I had been in love with for years was now the monster that I was trying to get away from. My body was only covered by a tank top, and I knew that I needed to throw some clothes on, but every time I tried to psych myself into getting up, I couldn't move. *Fuck it*, I thought to myself. I'd just wait for Knight to show up and see what happened. Using my phone, I called the number for the alarm system then keyed in a code that would open it so when he came, he would have no problem getting in.

It felt like hours later, even though it was only about twenty minutes. I heard a car pull up, and the screeching of the tires as it came to a stop. A door swung open, and I jumped up, and ran to the window to look out of it. The way the closet window was facing, I could see as Knight jumped out of his car and walked toward the door.

Seeing him, I knew that I was going to be okay. My body relaxed just from the sight of him.

Ding, dong!

The doorbell rang, and I heard the bed move as Tommy woke from his sleep.

"What the fuck!" he yelled out, then I heard his footsteps leaving from the room. "Grei!" he yelled as he headed down the stairs. I didn't know if he was going to look for me or answer the door, but I took this as my chance to put some clothes on. Quickly, I rummaged through the clothes and pulled out a pair of old jeans and a red shirt that I had left here. Most of my things were still at Farah's.

Pulling the jeans up over my wide hips, I wiggled to fit in because these shits were old jeans for a reason. I could still get them on, but not comfortably, so I never wore them. Throwing on the shirt, I slid into a pair of old PUMA slides. Opening the closet door, I made sure I had my phone before stepping out into the dark room. Walking toward the door, I tiptoed, trying to hear just what the fuck was going on.

Standing at the top of the stairs, I looked down at Knight and Tommy in a heated argument.

"Where the fuck is she at!" Knight yelled through gritted teeth. When we were together last night, he was so cool, so to see him like this was different. I didn't know if I should be scared of him or turned on.

"What you mean? Why the fuck you so worried about my bitch,

man?" Tommy asked him with his brows furrowed. They were pushed so closely together that he looked like he had a unibrow.

"Nigga, you must ain't get the fucking memo. That's my bitch now. Now, I told you before, don't put your fucking hands on her, so if she has so much as a fucking piece of hair out of place, I'mma kill you right here on the spot." Knight pulled his gun out and pointed it dead in Tommy's face.

Tommy stepped back and put his hands in the air. I would be scared shitless with a gun in my face, but he was standing tall and stoic. There wasn't a hint of nervousness in his demeanor.

"Nigga, speak up. You ain't gotta be scared to get ya fucking head blown off." Knight cocked the gun. "Grei!" he called, and with no thought at all, I started down the stairs as fast as I could in the slides I was wearing.

"Come into my eyesight." Knight didn't even look at me as he spoke. I walked closer so that he could get a good look at me.

He looked me up and down from head to toe, then back up again. His eyes stopped at my hair, and I patted it, suddenly feeling self-conscious. I knew that I looked a hot ass mess in these too tight jeans, raggedy shirt, and shoes with bed hair.

"What happened to your hair?" I hadn't looked in the mirror, but I could just imagine it was all over my head since Tommy dragged me by it.

"Uhm, nothing. I was just sleeping." Even though I wanted to be rid of Tommy, and even though he beat me like a bitch on the street, I still didn't want him to die. If he did die, then I didn't want it on my hands.

"You sure?" Knight asked. I looked at Tommy who still looked unbothered.

"Yes, I'm sure." My eyes moved over to Knight as I nodded my head. Slowly, he removed his gun from Tommy's face.

"Grei is now mine. Don't text her, call her, or try to get in touch with her. If I even find out you're so much as thinking about her, then I won't hesitate to kill you. Please, don't make me do to you what I did to ya brother." Since I had been down here, Tommy showed the first sign of emotion as his brows dipped like he was confused.

There was a smirk on Knight's face as he walked over to me, grabbed my hand, and walked with me toward the door. Once we got to the door, he turned around, and Tommy was standing there with a smug look on his face.

"Oh. You fired, my nigga. Hope you been saving some money to keep this rich ass lifestyle." He chuckled as he looked around the house. "If this shit wasn't a mockery of *Scarface*, then I would have bought it from you." Turning back toward me, he grabbed my hand and we got in the car.

The ride over to his house was quiet. I didn't know what he was thinking, but my life was heavily on my mind. How the hell could I go from my father treating me like a queen to letting a man treat me like shit? I wasn't one of those females who had a father that wasn't there. My father was actually a very important person in my life, and while I was growing up, we were so close.

As a little girl, at least once a month, my father would take me out on a date. He would spoil me and treat just how he said a man should treat me when I got older. My father would take me out to eat, to the movies, and he always made sure to open doors as well as pull out my chairs. I knew how I was supposed to be treated, so why did I allow Tommy to treat me like shit?

We pulled into the parking lot of Knight's condo, and he pulled into the same spot he had pulled into when I came here with him before. He pushed the engine button to turn the car off, but he didn't open the door. Looking over at him, he was looking at me with a face that I wasn't able to read.

"What happened?"

Shaking my head side to side, I told him exactly what went down from the time the Uber dropped me off outside of Farah's apartment to when he came and saved me. I skipped over the part about Tommy putting his hands on me and basically forcing me to have sex with him. If I told Knight the truth, I knew that he wouldn't hesitate to turn around and go back to the house to kill him.

"What made you call me?"

Looking him in the eyes, I spoke honestly.

"Well, first I called Farah, and she didn't answer. Then I called you and immediately felt some relief just from hearing your voice. I was happy that you answered, and I knew that you would save me. I don't know... There's just something about you." I couldn't believe that I was telling him this, but the way that I felt around him made me want to just tell him everything.

"Aight," was all he said as he opened the door and got out, leaving me wondering how he felt about what I had just said to him.

He opened my door, and I felt a certain type of way as I got out of the car. Walking ahead of him, I rolled my eyes into my head as I walked inside the building and the lobby. Standing in front of the elevators, I pushed the button without waiting for Knight.

Ding!

Just as the elevator doors opened, he was walking up to get on. I was hoping that he was walking too slow and missed the elevator. The elevator was empty as we both walked on. Knight hit the button for his floor, and we rode in silence once again. This was more awkward than the car though because now I felt like maybe he didn't really come and help me out.

He said that I was his though. Shaking my head, all I could think was, *silly me.* He was probably just saying that to get Tommy mad. Damn. What was that shit he said about Tommy being fired? Was he saying that Tommy was actually employed by him? My eyes widened just a bit as the realization hit me. That had to be what he was saying and why he said what he did at the pizza place that night.

The elevator dinged and opened as we reached his floor. I waited for him to step off first, but he put his arm out so that I could take the lead. There was a smirk on his face, so he was probably trying to be funny. We reached his door, and I stood there with my arms crossed while he unlocked it, using his handprint.

"I'll be right back!" Knight yelled back at me as he walked up the stairs of his condo. Slipping out of my slides, I walked into the living room area and looked out of the large window. You could see almost the entire downtown area from the window, and the view was amazing. My mind wandered as I looked at the vision in front of me.

There were so many people that were out living their lives. There were so many happy people in this city, and it sucked that I wasn't one of them. I wasn't doing what I loved, and the person that I had spent years with didn't make my heart skip a bit. If I was being honest, for the last couple of months, I had felt miserable.

Tommy literally sucked the life out of me, and it was going to take some time to get myself back how I used to be, but I was determined. Closing my eyes, I said a silent prayer to myself. I vowed to go back to my roots. Go back to the confident, happy woman who always had a smile on her face. I needed to get back to the me that knew her worth, and I was dead set on doing just that. I made a promise to myself that I knew I was going to keep; I had to keep it.

"What you thinking about?" Knight whispered in my ear as he wrapped his arms around me from the back.

My body melted into his instantly as if we were made just right for each other. He brought this feeling of relaxation over me that I had never felt before. I placed my arms over his and my hands on his hands.

"I'm just thinking about the girl I used to be. I feel like Tommy made me lose the person that I was, and I'm not proud of that."

"The woman that you are is not gone. You just have to realize that you deserve better, and bring that woman out. She's in there waiting; you just have to bring her out."

Nodding my head up and down, I agreed with him.

"You're right," I responded as a lone tear fell from my eye. Knight's hands were still on my waist as he turned me around to face him. I went to wipe the tear from my eye, but he grabbed my hand before I could reach my face.

"That tear right there is pain. Everybody gotta go through that shit, Grei, but only the strong ones survive." As he spoke, he looked into my eyes, and it was like I could feel everything he was saying to me. "Never let a nigga put they hands on you ever again. For one, you're too fucking beautiful, and for two—"

Cutting him off, I pressed my lips against his. He wrapped his arms around my waist and pulled me in closer to him. I wrapped my arms around Knight's neck, with my hands resting on the back of his neck. Knight was now rubbing and squeezing my ass in these too tight jeans. Breaking our kiss, he slapped my ass as he looked at me with his bottom lip tucked between his teeth.

"Don't start no shit you can't finish."

"Who says I can't finish it?" I sucked in my bottom lip and tilted my head to the right. A smirk spread across his face.

"You ain't ready for that shit, Grei. I'll fuck ya whole world up, ma." He stepped back and held my hand from afar. "Let me get you some clothes or some shit so you can take a shower."

Turning around, he went back up the stairs again. I felt like I had just got shut down but in a nice way. Knight said that he would fuck up my whole world, and if the dick could do that, then I wanted it. While he was upstairs looking for something I could wear, I went into the bathroom to start the shower.

His bathroom was nice as hell, just like the rest of his house. The first time I came here, I complimented him on having such good taste. The bathroom was navy blue, white, and silver. There was one wall painted blue while the other two walls were white. The sink was like a large bowl, and it was silver as well as the toothbrush holder, towels rods, and soap dish. Behind the door, there were a couple of silver shelves that held clean towels and washcloths.

The shower had a sliding door that was blue but had a light tint to it. It was transparent, so you could still see through it as you would if it was a clear sliding door. Sliding the door open, I started the water and easily got it to the perfect temperature. Knight was still upstairs, so I grabbed a towel and washcloth. I could just start my shower until he brought clothes down here.

Standing in the middle of the bathroom floor, I unbuckled my jeans and wiggled out of them as best as I could.

"Damn," I said aloud to myself. These jeans were so damn tight that they were still trying to cling to my thighs, even though I was trying to get them off.

Finally, they landed at the bottom of my feet, and I breathed a sigh of relief. Those damn jeans were going straight in the trash once I left out of this bathroom. Taking my shirt off, I let it hit the floor right on top of the jeans. I had already closed the bathroom door, so I slid the shower open and got in.

My eyes closed as I felt the hot water hit me. There was nothing like a hot ass shower that made the whole room drown in steam. The water crashed against my skin, and it was so refreshing after the long ass day that I had just endured.

"Ahhh!" I screamed as the shower door opened. There stood Knight in nothing at all.

"What? You were all over me just a couple of minutes ago, but now I can't get in?"

I couldn't answer him because my voice was stuck in my throat. His dick being out had my brain all fucked up. It was like I wanted to have a good comeback, but I couldn't even talk, even though I was fully capable.

"Uhhh, sure," I finally got out. Knight did a low laugh as he shook his head and got in behind me.

Knight moved up and stood beside me. There was enough room in his shower for us to stand next to each other rather than one behind the other. I was trying not to look, but my eyes were pulled toward it. His dick was semi-hard, and it was the biggest dick I had ever seen. It was even bigger than the men in the pornos I'd watched when masturbating while Tommy was away.

It had to be about ten inches, and I was not overexaggerating. It wasn't just long, but it was thick too. Knight's dick put Tommy's to shame and would have his ass hiding in a closet somewhere. I also noticed that he didn't have that big bush of pubic hair. Him shaving was a plus. I swear I hated giving Tommy head. There would be hair on my tongue or getting stuck between my teeth.

"Don't just stare at it; touch it." Knight was standing there with his legs spread apart and a sexy but serious look on his face. He wasn't into playing games, and I knew that about him just from the little bit of time that we had spent together.

Fuck it, I thought as I reached out my hand and wrapped it around the shaft of his dick. I started to jack it slowly, moving my hand up and down. His dick was so smooth, and it looked even better as it came alive. Looking into his eyes, he was watching me with his bottom lip tucked in between his teeth.

His chocolate ass looked so damn sexy, and in that moment, I really didn't care what he would think about me tomorrow. I didn't care if he thought I was a hoe, and I didn't care if tomorrow we parted ways, because all I cared about was this moment. Right then, in my mind, I made myself a promise: to get nasty as hell with him and do everything that I'd always wanted to do. All the things I had fantasized about but knew Tommy wasn't the man to get the job done.

KNIGHT

Grei was looking at my dick like she wanted to jump on it, and shit, if that's what she wanted to do, then I wasn't going to stop her at all. By the window, I was trying to be a gentleman because she had been through a lot tonight, but once I walked into this bathroom and saw her naked silhouette through the glass door, I just couldn't help myself. Those thick ass thighs and her perfect sized breasts had a nigga's dick getting hard before she even touched me.

As if she finally decided to go for it, Grei dropped down to her knees and wasted no time wrapping her mouth around my dick. Her mouth was warm and wet as fuck, making me bite my bottom lip. Looking down at Grei, she was looking up at me as she bobbed up and down. Both of her hands were wrapped around my shaft. She was jacking it with both hands and making it wet at the same time.

"Yeah, suck that shit."

My hand was on the back of her head. When I pushed her head down, my dick touched the back of her throat, making her gag. Grei pulled back a little bit to get herself together then deep throated again. She gagged again, and it sounded sexy as hell. With both eyes looking up at me, she put her right hand on my balls and rubbed them while she sucked my dick with no hands.

"Mmmm," she moaned, and that shit sent me over the edge. I started cumming, and I was happy she wasn't one of those "I don't swallow cum" bitches. She sucked me dry and then made sure my soul had left from my body.

I went to turn the shower off when she stopped me.

"Knight, I still have to take a shower," she laughed.

"Shit. That head made a nigga forget why the fuck we were in here." I wasn't a nigga that needed pussy, so the fact Grei had me forgetting shit had to be something else.

We both washed up and got out of the shower. She grabbed a towel that she had taken out of the linen closet, and I grabbed my towel that was hanging on the towel rail. We were both standing in front of the mirror as we dried off. Grei was focused on her body as she dried off, and I was looking at her. She was really beautiful as hell.

"What?" she asked as she paused with the towel covering her body like I hadn't already seen everything there was possible to see.

"Just admiring how beautiful you are." A smile spread across her face as she blushed. "Nah, I'm just fucking with you. You got a booger in ya nose," I said with a serious face, wrapped the towel around me, and walked out of the bathroom.

She didn't really have a booger, but I wasn't trying to have her thinking that she was the shit. Walking upstairs, I could hear her feet hit the hardwood floors as she followed behind me.

"You're an asshole, Knight."

"Lay down on the bed," I ordered her as we walked into my room.

"What?" She stopped in her tracks like she hadn't heard what I had just said.

"Grei, I know you didn't think you was going to suck my dick like that and I wouldn't get you back. Lay that ass down on the bed, on ya back, and spread your legs open."

Grei looked at me, and I matched her stare. I wasn't about to play with her ass, and she needed to know that a nigga was serious.

GREI

I stopped in place and looked at him to see if he was serious, and I didn't see a hint of this being a joke. Of course, I knew we were going to have sex tonight, but I didn't know he was going to be so demanding. Maybe I should have known from his whole demeanor that was how he was going to be. Walking over to the bed, I dropped the towel and did as Knight told me.

I laid on my back in the middle of his California king size bed and spread my legs open. I was thanking God that I had been getting my Brazilian waxes on schedule because my shit was still nice and smooth. Knight walked over and stood at the end of the bed.

"Play with that pussy."

Using my right hand, I traveled down my torso to my pussy. Usually, I would be doing this while home alone. Spreading my lips with my pointer and ring fingers, I used my middle finger to rub my clit. With each rub, my pussy got wetter. Knight dropped the towel, and seeing his dick turned me on even more.

When he came in my mouth, it was sweet, like he only ate fruit and drank water. His dick grew as he stroked it slowly.

"Make that pussy cum for daddy."

Throwing my head back, I closed my eyes as I felt myself about to erupt.

"Oh fuckkkk," I moaned out loud. I came all over the bed.

"Come here." Knight patted the end of the bed that was right in front of where he was standing. I scooted down to the designated spot, and he bent down on his knees right in front of me. He got low enough that he was eye level with my pussy.

Knight hooked both of my legs with his arms and pulled me to him, putting my pussy on his mouth. His mouth was right on my clit, sucking and licking it. His tongue flicked back and forth over my swollen nub.

"Oooo, right there, right there." My hand was on the back of his head, unsure if I wanted to pull him in or push him away. Looking down at him, he was looking up at me. Once our eyes locked, his tongue started to move faster, and I knew I was going to cum soon.

"Mmmm, uh, mmmm." My breathing started to speed up as well as my moans. "I'm comingggggggg." I released and came all in his mouth. His mustache and beard instantly became saturated with my juices.

"Okay, I'm done. I'm done, I'm done." I tried to push his head back, but he didn't budge.

"Nah, one more. You can get one more out."

"No, I ca—" Before I could get the complete sentence out, his mouth was latched back onto my pussy.

"Please, st-stop. Baby, please." My clit was so sensitive to the touch. He was eating my pussy like he hadn't eaten in days. His arms were locked around my legs, holding me in place. I tried to push his head back, but he wasn't letting up, so I just gave up.

Tears started to come out of my eyes, and it wasn't because of pain; it was all pleasure. I could feel my soul lifting from my body.

"Knight, wait. I gotta pee. I gotta pee." I tried to pull away from him, but he still didn't budge. "Pleaseeee, I gotta pee."

I felt the urge to pee, and I knew that he knew what I was saying because he was looking right at me. There was no way he couldn't hear me.

"Ahhhhh!"

As soon as I started cumming, Knight moved back, and I squirted all over the side of the bed. It dripped down the side of the bed and onto the floor. My chest heaved up and down as I tried to catch my breath. That was the best orgasm that I had ever had in my life.

"Get ya shit together; we ain't done yet." Knight chuckled and slapped my thigh. "Lay in the middle of the bed."

I half wanted to run out of his room and hide somewhere because I didn't know how much more I could handle, but there was no way I wasn't about to sample that dick. It was so thick that the veins were poking out. His dick looked like it was on steroids and about to bust if he didn't cum soon. Knight pushed both of my legs up and put his dick at the tip of my slit.

"Breathe, mama."

I exhaled, not even realizing that I was holding my breath.

"Okay," I spoke, letting him know I was ready and relaxed. I was acting like I was a virgin, but I had never had sex with a man whose dick was this big.

Knight started to push his way in. Inch by inch, he slowly pushed his dick inside of me.

"Damn, this shit tight as fuck."

It felt like he was ripping me in half, but I knew the pleasure would start soon.

"Almost in."

Less than a minute later, the pain turned into pleasure, and I was back revived. He was hitting my spot; hitting it every time he stroked inside of me. I had never felt a nigga in my guts before, but this nigga was in my guts! Knight pumped in and out of me with my legs up on his shoulders.

"Yessss. That feels so fucking good." My body shuddered, and I came on his dick.

Without saying a word, Knight slipped his dick out of me and turned me over in one motion. Pushing my back, I arched it just right so that my ass was up and face was down. Knight slid his dick inside me again, and my pussy sucked it in like it was a vacuum. There was zero pain and nothing but undeniable pleasure.

Whap!

Knight slapped my ass, and I could feel the sting.

Whap!

"Ya ass so fat." Both hands were on my ass as he squeezed it. "Come here."

Grabbing my arms, he lifted me up and started to pump his dick in and out of me. One hand was wrapped around my hair, and the other hand was wrapped around my neck. The tighter he squeezed, the more turned on I got.

"Shit, I'm about to cum. Cum for me, Grei." Yanking my head to the right by my hair, he bit down on the left side of my neck. My pussy clenched onto his dick, and my juices leaked all over it. When we were done, I could feel his dick thumping inside of me.

"Knight, we didn't use a condom."

"It's cool. We'll go get a Plan B in the morning." Pulling out of me, he rolled over and laid on his back. Looking at him, his dick was hard again. I looked from his dick to his face, which had a cocky smirk on it.

"Don't just look at it. Ride that shit."

My legs were weak, and I felt like I couldn't cum anymore. His dick was too good though, and I knew another dose would put me to sleep. Getting on top of him, I slid his dick in and started to ride it like this was the last time.

TRELL

*S*hit was going good, and for that, a nigga couldn't complain. I mean, it could have been better, but I was grinding my ass off until me and my lil' lady wanted for nothing. The streets were all I knew, and it was where I grew up. My momma still lived in the projects, and I didn't stay that far away. I was stacking my money up and planning on moving us all out the hood soon. My lil' lady and my momma were my world, and I wanted to make sure they were straight.

Pulling into the parking lot of the housing projects my mom lived in, I pulled into a spot that was right in front of my momma's crib. It was late as hell, and I had been at the trap all day, making sure shit was straight. I was cool with being in charge, and I always knew that nigga Dallas wasn't cut for being a leader. That nigga was weak as fuck, and I knew he was a fucking thief. He was always doing some lil' slick shit, but I was always on guard, and I paid attention to everything, even the smallest detail.

Cutting the engine, I stepped out of my 2012 Honda Accord. It wasn't the hottest car, but a nigga like me didn't care about that shit. I didn't care about driving the best car or wearing Gucci and all that other brand name shit. My mind was set on securing the future and getting to the bag. Knight had given me my chance to do just that.

Knight was a cool nigga from what I could see, but I hadn't been around him much. Shit, I didn't even know Tommy's ass either. It was like nobody came to check on shit. You would think that a nigga would come check up on his spots, but that nigga Tommy was just as goofy as his damn brother. I saw his ass once in a blue moon, and he didn't do shit but come around and flex. I was surprised we were still able to even make money with a half-ass leader.

My black Air Max hit the pavement as I walked to my mother's front door and stuck the key in. Just as I opened the door, the sounds of my lady crying invaded my ears. Closing the door behind myself, I walked through the small hallway and into the kitchen where I saw a light shining. Walking in, a smile instantly spread across a nigga's face.

"Lil' lady, what you doing up?" I talked to my daughter as I grabbed her from my mother's arms.

My lil' lady was my five-month-old daughter, Layla. She was the most important person in my life besides my mom. I held her in my arms as she cried, but not as loud since she heard my voice. Layla poked her lip out, and I couldn't help but to hold her closer.

"Awww, Grandma playing with your food, baby girl? You hungry?" Holding her on my shoulder, I rubbed her back in a circular motion.

"Whew! That child got a set of lungs on her." My mother shook her head from side to side as she spoke and held on to the counter as if she was balancing herself. Her eyes were barely open, and I knew she was tired as hell.

My mother was my heart, and after my father died when I was five, she raised me on her own. Working two jobs and barely being able to see me, she had to sacrifice just to take care of me. She was a strong woman, and I was glad that she was able to keep my daughter while I got shit right. I made sure her bills were paid so she didn't have to work, and in return, she made sure my shorty was good. It wasn't about the money for her though, because she would keep Layla for free.

"Ma, go ahead to bed. I got this, and I can lock up when we leave."

"Okay." She didn't try to protest. She just walked up the stairs to go to bed. Still bouncing my lil' lady on my shoulder, I walked to the cup that was holding hot water and her bottle. Taking it out, I opened the top and tested it out on my wrist. It was perfect, so I held her in my arms and popped it in her mouth. Layla started sucking like she hadn't eaten in days, and I knew my momma didn't starve her little ass.

Layla was already dressed in a pink and yellow butterfly one piece that covered the feet and all. I walked into the living room and flipped the switch to turn the light on. Putting her in her car seat, I grabbed a blanket and put it under her bottle to prop it up. Her eyes were half closed as she continued to suck on the bottle.

Walking around the living room, I grabbed her bag, blankets, rattles, and everything else that was around the room. It was a warm night, so I didn't have to put a jacket or anything on Layla; just put a blanket over her. Once I had everything together, I picked up Layla, turned the light off, and we headed out of the house. This is how most, if not all of my days went. Working, then going to pick up my baby girl and heading home.

Our apartment was only five minutes away from my mother's house. It was still in the hood, but it wasn't bad. This shit wasn't ideal, but pretty soon, I would be looking for a bigger house in a nicer area. I just had to keep grinding and keep my eyes on the bigger picture. We lived on the fourth floor of a building with about thirty apartments.

The car was silent because I hadn't put the radio on as we pulled into the parking lot and into my designated spot. That was one of the things I liked about living here was the designated parking spot. My shit was right by the door because me and the owner of the building had a little arrangement. Twisting the key in the ignition, the engine stopped, and I made sure my gun was in my waist before getting out of the car. There was no way I was going to be caught lacking, especially when my lil' lady was with me.

I got out and opened the back door, and my baby was knocked out. That bottle was all that she needed. Grabbing her car seat, I carried her out of the car and into the building. The elevators were right inside the lobby, so I didn't have to carry her far. We got on, and I pushed the button for the fourth floor. The doors closed almost automatically, and the elevator started going up.

Ding!

When the doors opened, I walked off and toward the left where my apartment was. I had been living in this building for a little over a year now, ever since Layla's mother was pregnant with her. Pulling my key out of my front pants pocket, I unlocked the door and pushed it open. As soon as the door was open, I put my left hand out and hit the switch, lighting up the living room.

Walking into the house, I slammed the door shut with my foot, and it closed harder than I thought it would. Looking down at Layla, she moved a little, but her eyes stayed closed. Some nights she was a heavy sleeper, but most nights, the slightest noise would have my lil' lady up. I thanked God she didn't wake up because a nigga was tired. I loved chilling with Layla, but a nigga had a long ass day.

Our apartment wasn't big, but it wasn't small either. It was a two-bedroom apartment with a living room/dining area and a small ass kitchen. There was a small hallway where the rooms and bathroom were. Turning down the hallway, I turned the light on, walked past the first room, and inside the second, which was Layla's room. Her night-light was still plugged on from last night, so the room was illuminated enough.

I set her car seat on the carpeted floor next to her crib. Making sure her blankets were just right in the crib, I unbuckled her safety belt and scooped her up. She didn't open an eye as I laid her down in the crib. Kissing her on the forehead, I walked out of her room and into mine.

"What the fuck!" I yelled out as I switched on my light and pulled my gun out of my waist. "What the fuck you doing in my shit?"

She had a stuck expression on her face like she didn't know I was going to react this way. Maybe she thought that the hot pink lingerie she had on was going to keep me from acting a fool, but that was a damn lie. My gun was still pointed at her.

"I-I was trying to surprise you." Her lips trembled as she spoke.

"I've told you before not to come in my fucking apartment unannounced. You the landlord, nothing more. We fuck, but that's it, so I don't know why the fuck you keep trying to surprise me like you my bitch." I was fuming now and trying not to scream because I didn't want to wake Layla. "Get up."

Slowly, she lifted herself from the bed and stood up in the hot pink stilettos she was wearing. Her legs wobbled a bit, but then she was able to stand up steady. I didn't know if it was because of the gun I still had pointed or the fact that her dogs were obviously screaming to get out of those damn shoes. Dayja wasn't a fat chick, but she was thick, and her feet looked like they were stuffed inside the shoe.

"Get out. If you come back again, we gon' have a problem." My voice was low, but she knew that I wasn't fucking around as she scurried out of the room, and two seconds later, I heard the front door close. Finally, I let my hand holding the gun drop down to my side. I was changing my fucking locks tomorrow, landlord or not. I couldn't wait to get the fuck up outta here, because I didn't like muthafuckas knowing where I rested my head at.

FARAH

*I*t had been a week since I left Grei at the bar with Knight, and today was the first day that I would be seeing her. She had called me, inviting me to lunch because she needed to talk to me about something. It was probably going to be about how that nigga had her head over heels, because she hadn't been back to the house at all. Two days after the bar, I called to check up on her, and she said she was fine, and things were good.

Opening the door to The Cheesecake Factory, I walked over to the hostess. Grei had already texted me to let me know that she was here and seated. There were a couple of people sitting in the waiting area, waiting for a table, and there was one face in particular that stood out to me. He was standing beside a beautiful woman, and they looked like the perfect couple.

He looked like a Ken doll, and she looked like Malibu Barbie. When his eyes met mine, his face immediately turned a bright red. I didn't know whether he was afraid I was going to say something or blushing because I was looking fine as hell. I was wearing a pair of red and black tie-dye flare pants that hugged my curves, with a matching crop top and a pair of black sandals. Walking past him as if I didn't even know him, I walked up to the hostess.

"Welcome to The Cheesecake Factory. How can I help you?" She was short and bubbly with blonde hair and blue eyes.

"I'm looking for my friend. She already got seated and let you guys know that I would be coming."

"Oh yeah. Follow me this way."

She turned around, and I followed behind her and her bouncy blonde hair that was pulled into a high ponytail. Looking back, I caught the familiar face staring at my ass, and I couldn't do nothing but shake my head. We didn't have to walk far until I saw Grei with her head all in her phone and a big ass smile on her face.

"You must be talking to Knight," I said as I sat down, and the hostess walked away after telling us our server would be right with us.

"Hey, Farah." She typed something in her phone then put it down. "Why you say that?"

"Because I walked up and you were smiling like you hit the lottery. I've never seen you with this glow on your face that you have now." She was looking pretty as hell and was still smiling. Grei had her naturally curly hair pulled into a bun. She was wearing a pair of gold hoop earrings and had on a red and white striped shorts romper with a red clutch purse.

"Whatever." She laughed and waved me off but didn't deny that it was him.

"Hello, my name is Ashley, and I'll be your server today." A waitress walked up to our table. She was just as perky as the hostess. "Can I start you two off with drinks?"

"Water with lemon," Grei ordered.

"I'll have a margarita," I ordered with a smile as I pulled my ID from my purse and flashed it. After taking our drink orders, she walked away to get them and give us time to look at the menu. I had been here a couple of times before, so I already knew what I wanted and didn't have to look.

"So, what's been going on with you? I see the glow, so that's a good thing, but what did you have to tell me?"

"Farah, so much has happened. First off, where the hell have you been? I called you the next day after you left the bar, and you didn't answer. I thought you were off work?"

"I was, but the damn relief didn't show up, so I ended up having to stay, and my phone died." It was way too easy for me to come up with these lies to cover myself.

"Girl, shit got real." The smile dropped from her face as she shook her head from side to side.

"How? What happened?" I leaned forward in my seat.

"Here are your drinks." The waitress interrupted and placed our drinks down in front of us. "Are you ready to order, or do you need me to come back?"

"We're ready," Grei answered her and started to order. "I'll have the grilled turkey burger, no onions or tomatoes."

"And are the French fries fine with that?"

"Yes."

"Okay, and what would you like?" She looked at me with a smile.

"I'll have the Chinese chicken salad with extra chicken and ranch dressing."

"Okay, I'll put that in for you two." She walked away, and I looked right back at Grei, waiting for her to finish telling me the story.

She wasted no time telling me all about the night at the bar and then the day after. When she started telling me about what Tommy did to her, I could feel the warm tears filling the pools of my eyes. I knew that he wasn't shit, but I didn't know that for years he had been putting his hands on her and doing everything but tying her down to basically force her to have sex with him. I didn't care if technically he was her "boyfriend", that was rape, and that nigga was a coward.

Tommy may have had a name in these streets because he had money, but I had never heard about that nigga busting a grape in a fruit fight. The fact that he could put his hands on my cousin but not one of these niggas, was proof enough that he was a bitch.

"Once he fell asleep, that's when I called you, but you didn't answer, so I had to call Knight. Thank God I had my phone because I wouldn't have been able to remember his number, and who knows what would have happened." Suddenly, I felt guilty for not being available.

"So, ummm, what did Knight do?"

"Girl, I knew that nigga was crazy because I had heard all of the stories about him, but I didn't know just how crazy he really was. He came in there, pulled a gun on Tommy, and got me out of there. Shit was crazy, but I'm happy to just finally be away from him."

"Here's the burger, and here's the salad. Is there anything else I can get you two?" The waitress set our plates in front of each of us. I scanned the table to make sure there were extra napkins and that I had enough dressing. Both were good.

"We're fine," Grei and I answered her at the same time, and she walked away.

"So what's your plan now?" I asked her as I poured the dressing onto my salad.

"Welll, Knight wants me to stay with him, and I want to, but I don't know. I don't want to go from depending on one man to another, you know?"

"I get it. If you want, you can stay at my house as long as you want or need to. I've always wanted a roommate." I spoke with a bright smile on my face.

"I think that's what I'm going to do. I'll wait until after the weekend and let him know. Speaking of the weekend." Grei looked at me with a grin on her face. "You have any plans?"

"No. Probably just do some laundry. Why, what's up?"

"Knight is throwing some dude name Trell a party at the club. You should come."

"I will be there. I don't have shit else to do."

"Okay. I have to go to the mall when I leave here and find something to wear."

"I have a couple of outfits I just got from Fashion Nova, so I can wear one of those. I'll go with you to the mall though." I didn't have anything else to do, and I hadn't really been able to spend any time with Grei. Tommy really kept her away from us, and I had missed the hell out of her.

"No rush at all, but your bill has been paid by the gentleman over there." The waitress stood at the end of our table and pointed across the room then walked away after leaving the receipt on the table. We looked, and there was the familiar face. The woman he was with wasn't at the table, so she must have been in the bathroom or something. He looked over at me and smiled then winked.

"Who is that?" Grei asked.

"I don't know. Probably just someone doing a good deed." I turned away from him and to her. "What mall are you going to?" I needed to change the subject because there was no way that I would be able to tell her just how I knew the man across the room.

KNIGHT

The club was packed as hell tonight. I had told all my niggas to come out tonight because we were celebrating. Just a lil' celebration for Trell being in charge instead of that fuck ass nigga Dallas, also me being in the forefront running my business as me and not playing the background. They didn't know it yet, but I was about to announce myself boss and let these niggas know just what the fuck it was.

Our VIP was hype as fuck with nothing but real niggas and a couple of bitches. Of course, Grei was on the left of me as she sipped on a glass of Belaire. She wasn't paying me any attention as she talked to her cousin Farah that was sitting next to her. Grei was looking good as fuck tonight, and I couldn't wait to get her back to the crib.

"Yo, what's good?" Trell walked up and slapped me up. This nigga was basically the guest of honor but was just getting his ass here.

"What's up?" I dapped him up. "What, you had to make a grand entrance, nigga?" I joked.

"Nah, I had to get my daughter ready for bed and all that."

"Word. How baby girl doing?"

"She good. You know, growing every day and all that shit."

"You don't gotta go get her tonight, right?" I asked because we were about to get fucked up.

"Hell nah, nigga. You throwing a nigga a lil' celebration and shit. I'mma get fucked up."

Before he could even finish his statement, I already had a bottle of D'USSÉ in my hand and handed it to him. Tonight was definitely about to be one for the books.

"Bae." Grei spoke into my ear so that I could hear her over the music, and I wrapped my arms around her, pulling her in closer. "Me and Farah about to run to the bathroom real quick."

"'light." I nodded my head. They both got up and headed toward the VIP entrance, and I watched her backside as she started to walk through the crowd.

"Yo, she not gonna get kidnapped going to the bathroom, you in love ass nigga." Cruz laughed as he walked over to me with a blunt in his hand. He was at the other end of VIP with a couple of bitches I had seen around the hood before. They were the type of bitches that got grazed with bullets and would rat on a nigga if he did her wrong. They weren't the type of bitches you trust.

"What's up?" Cruz slapped up Trell that was now sitting a little far down on the right side of me on the couch. He was nodding his head to the beat as he scanned the crowd. That was how I knew that making him a leader was the right decision. He was always on his toes and watching his surroundings, making sure shit was cool, even when we were just chilling.

Turning my attention back to Cruz, I waved my hand at his ass as I spoke.

"Nigga, shut yo' ass up. I'm making sure mines good, nigga," I said, referring to Grei.

"Damn, you claiming shorty already? That pussy must be good then," Cruz said with a smirk on his face as he passed me the blunt he was smoking. I took it from him but looked at him with a serious expression on my face. Looking him directly in the eye, I talked to the nigga so that he knew I was serious.

"Don't say no shit like that, yo. Don't even mention her pussy. Her pussy should never be a concern of yours. That's not some random bitch; that's going to be my wife." I put the blunt to my lips and inhaled.

"My bad," he said as he held his hands up in surrender. "But how that nigga Tommy taking it? You know he love that bit—I mean, Grei." Cruz caught himself.

"Fuck that nigga. If he knows what's good for him, he'll take that L and leave that shit alone." Taking another pull from the blunt, I handed it back to Cruz then sat back.

Just as I sat back, Grei walked up and sat on my lap. The yellow dress that she was wearing barely covered up her thick ass thighs. Leaning into me, she grabbed both sides of my face and kissed me on the lips.

"You are so handsome," she spoke as she bit her bottom lip and smiled at me.

"You're sexy as fuck, and I can't wait to get you home and fuck the shit out of you." My left hand was on her thigh as I squeezed it.

"Mmm, I can't wait." She leaned into me again, and we started to kiss. Being in the club kissing was different for me, but with Grei, it felt so natural.

My hand continued to roam up her thigh and to her smooth pussy. It was warm and wet as I opened it slightly and rubbed her nub. Grei leaned in and laid her head on my shoulder. Parting her lower lips, I started to rub her clit.

"Baby, you're going to make me cum," she moaned.

Her lips latched onto my neck, and she started to suck hard as hell. I knew I was going to have a damn hickey when we left this club. Rubbing faster, I knew that Grei was about to have an orgasm because of the way she moaned.

"Fuck, fuck, fuck." Just as the last fuck came out of her mouth, she was cumming all over my fingers.

FARAH

$\mathcal{I}$ was on my phone taking Snapchat pictures with filters, but in my peripheral, I could see Grei and Knight basically almost fucking. She would never have been all over Tommy like she was Knight, and I was happy as hell for her. Like I told her at lunch, she had this crazy glow to her now, and I was feeling it. It was great to see my cousin so happy.

Looking around the VIP area, my eyes laid on the light-skinned nigga. He was a loudmouth and was hype as hell. That was the most unattractive thing to me in a man. I hated the loud types that needed attention and wanted all eyes to be on them. He was cute, but he just wasn't my type.

My eyes continued to scan around VIP and landed on a guy that was sexy as hell, and he had a rugged look to him. He was sitting on the other side of the couch, drinking out of a bottle of D'USSÉ. He was wearing a red and black Polo shirt with a pair of dark blue jeans on. When I walked past him, I saw that he was wearing a pair of black and red Jordans on his feet. I didn't know the number or anything because I didn't know sneakers like that.

Getting up, I smoothed out the fire red dress that I was wearing and walked toward the man with the D'USSÉ. I already knew that my hair and lips were on point because I had double checked everything while I was in the bathroom. My hand was grabbed from behind me, preventing me from making it to my destination. I turned around, and it was the light-skinned loud mouth with a blunt hanging out of his mouth.

"What's up, ma? Why you leaving?" He looked me up and down like I was a ribeye steak fresh off the grill.

"First off, my name is not ma. Second, get ya hands off me." Pulling my hand from him, I walked away and headed to where I was going in the first place.

Walking up on him, he was even cuter than what he looked like from afar. His brown skin complexion was perfect, and he didn't have a blemish in sight. His brush cut was fresh as if he had just come from the barber shop before coming here. I wasn't the shy type at all, so I had no problem introducing myself to him and sparking a conversation.

"Hey, what's your name?" I asked him with a smile on my face and my head tilted to the right.

His eyes matched mine. They were low as he looked me up and down before replying. Even though asking his name was such a simple question, it could lead the conversation to a million different places, and that's all I needed.

"What? Why you want to know my name?"

"Because you're a handsome man, and I've always been attracted to the cool and quiet type." Laughing, he sat back on the couch and spread his legs apart.

"Trell. What's your name?"

"Farah. Do you mind if I sit with you? It's kind of boring taking pictures on my phone while my cousin and Knight damn near fuck next to me." I pointed to a Grei that was now laying nestled on Knight's shoulder like she had just had the best orgasm ever.

Looking back at Trell, we both laughed because we were both thinking the same thing. Her face told it all.

"That's cool."

I accepted the half invitation and went ahead and sat down next to him. As soon as I sat next to him, a scent hit my nose. This man smelled good as fuck, like whatever scent he had on him made bitches want to jump right on his lap and start fucking him. It made my insides tingle and made me want to be that bitch.

"So, aren't you the one who this party is for?" When I heard his name, I remembered Grei mentioning the party was for a dude named Trell. She didn't mention how sexy Trell was.

"Yeah," he responded nonchalantly.

I could tell the type that Trell was, and I didn't know if he was a nigga that I would be interested in messing with. I loved the quiet type, but this nigga was too quiet. He wasn't even trying to hold a conversation with me even after I had initiated it. Maybe he just wasn't interested, but the way I looked in this dress, there was no way he wasn't attracted to me.

Doing what I do for a living, I was able to label people off the bat. It wasn't a bad thing, but it also wasn't necessarily good. It was now a habit for me to prejudge people from just a couple of sentences of conversation.

"Okay, that's cool." I sat back and pulled my phone out. If I got a reaction, then he was interested, but if I got nothing, then I might as well go back and sit next to the couple that were damn near fucking in the middle of VIP.

"How you going to come sit over here with me and you got ya phone out?" Trell spoke in his sexy ass voice. I didn't know what it was, but everything about this man was fine. He just had this aura about him.

Thirty minutes later, Trell and I were talking like we had been friends forever. He was actually funny as hell, and I loved a nigga with humor. I didn't know if he was usually this cool or if it was the liquor and weed making him friendly.

"So you really think Chris Rock was better than Chris Tucker in his prime?" he asked me again.

"Yesss. Chris Rock is really funny as hell." I stuck by my answer. I didn't even remember how we had gotten to this conversation, but we had been discussing actors and comedians for the last five minutes.

"Nah, he cool and all, but he not funnier than Chris Tucker in his prime, man. You wilding, Farah." Trell puffed on the blunt he was smoking and passed it to me. In the midst of talking, Trell had pulled out some weed and a blunt and started rolling up.

I wasn't a big smoker, but on occasion, I would. I never went past one blunt though, because I would get high way too quick. Taking the blunt from his hand, I took a pull from it and felt my high immediately boost. Whatever weed he was smoking was strong as fuck.

"No! Let me through! Fuck that! That's my baby daddy, and I need to talk to him!"

Almost everybody in VIP turned their head toward the entrance. There was a woman at the entrance yelling, trying to get past security.

"Trell! Trell, tell him to let me in!" she yelled, and I looked from her to him. I didn't really care that he had a baby or baby momma, but she was embarrassing, and I hoped she wasn't trying to start some shit, because I would hate to have to whoop ass over a nigga I was not even fucking—hadn't even exchanged numbers, let alone stares.

Trell nodded his head toward security, and they let her in. Once she walked in, everybody went back to what they were doing because there obviously wasn't going to be a fight or any more of a problem. She started toward Trell with eyes so small they looked like daggers. At least he didn't have an ugly baby mother. The only thing that I saw wrong with her was the forty-inch hair down to her ass. Like, honey, why was hair that long necessary?

"So you can't invite your baby mother out now?" Her hand was on her hip, and her neck rolled like a snake.

"Yo, Tonya, don't do that. Don't show out, 'cause I would hate to have to embarrass you in here. Take ya hand off ya fucking hip, and don't move ya neck when you fucking talking to me."

Immediately, her hand fell from her hip, and she straightened up. It was like her whole persona changed after he spoke.

"Now, what do you want?" he asked her, his eyes drilling into her.

"I just wanted to know why you didn't invite me? We may not be together, but you can still invite me to a party that's for you." Watching this shit in front of me, it was hard not to laugh. First, she was coming in here like she wanted smoke, and now she was trying to talk like her ass had some sense.

"That's all you wanted?"

"Yeah." Her body relaxed a bit.

"So you made a fucking scene to come ask me why you weren't invited to a party? You're not going to ask about your five-month-old daughter and how she's doing!" His voice was raised, but because of the music, there wasn't that much attention to the two. "Layla ain't seen ya dumb ass in months. She probably thinks my fucking momma is her momma, but you talking to me about a fucking party?"

Trell's lips were turned up in disgust as he looked her up and down. She seemed to just about crumble under his scrutiny.

"H-how is she?" she stuttered.

"Don't worry about it. Get the fuck from around me."

"Trell, don't—"

"Don't what? Treat you like the fucking dead-beat mother that you are? Treat you like a bitch that doesn't even call or see her child?"

"Don't treat me like I don't love Layla." Tears started to come out of her eyes.

At this point, the blunt had gone out, my phone was down, and I was watching this scene in front of me like it was a movie. I couldn't believe that this conversation was happening inside of a club right now, and I was the one witnessing it. I kept looking around to see if anybody was seeing it, but it was like I was the only one able to see this.

"Fuck you and them fake ass tears. You don't care about anybody but ya self. You ain't nothing but a hoe ass, dead-beat ass mom. Now get the fuck out my face like I said." Trell looked at her like she was covered in shit.

Tonya said nothing as she turned around and walked away with her head down. She continued out of VIP and maybe out of the club. Shit, I would be running for the door after the shit that he had just said to her. Trell got up and walked over to Knight. They talked for a minute before dapping up, the signature greeting and farewell.

"I'm out. It was cool meeting you, shorty. Enjoy ya night," he spoke to me as he walked right past, not even offering a hug, handshake, or his number. I wasn't used to men not taking the initiative or trying to talk to me. Trell was different.

GREI

"You ready?" Knight whispered in my ear then looked at me.

"Yes," I responded while nodding my head up and down with a smile on my face. I was ready to finish what Knight had already started, and I wasn't sure if we were even going to make it home. I was ready to jump on his ass as soon as we got in the car.

Knight put his hand out, and I placed my hand in his as I stood up from the couch. As we walked out, he said bye and nodded his head toward a couple of people. He wasn't being all extra how Tommy was, and he wasn't giving any bitch that was staring us down any attention at all. This felt so different and so much more securing than when I went anywhere with Tommy.

Outside of the club, we walked across the street to the parking lot where we had parked. There were about twenty to thirty people outside of the club, getting ready for the club to close, better known as the let out. If you didn't go to the club, you could still come down here to see and talk to everybody that was inside the club. We reached Knight's car, and he opened the door for me. I slid on the seats, and he closed the door behind me.

Just as he was about to get in the car, his homeboy Cruz was jogging across the street. Instead of opening his door, he met him on the sidewalk, and they talked. Cruz seemed cool from what Knight had told me about him, but what I learned about him tonight was he was a loud mouth. That was the worst type of nigga to be besides a thief and a rat. My father instilled that in me my whole life.

Buzz, buzz!

My phone vibrated, and it was a message from Farah telling me that she had just got home. A little after Trell told Knight he was leaving, Farah left as well. I saw them talking while we were chilling, and they looked like they were having a good time. Maybe that could potentially be something.

Just as I looked up from the phone, Knight was walking toward the car, and Cruz was going back to the club.

"My bad," Knight said as he sat in his seat and closed the door. He started the car and pulled out of the parking lot. The radio was on, playing a throwback, "Sex" by Jamie Foxx. Sex was already on my mind, and this wasn't making it any better.

With no hesitation, I turned to Knight and started to unbuckle his pants. He didn't protest at all as he assisted me with pulling his jeans down and pulling his dick through the slit in his boxers. It wasn't an easy task, but once his dick was out, the award was much greater than the task. I wasted no time wrapping my lips around his dick.

I was still sitting in my seat but was leaning over the armrest and to the left. It wasn't exactly comfortable, but that was the least of my worries. Getting as much as I could of him in my mouth as possible, I deep throated his dick.

"Shit!" he yelled out.

I couldn't deep throat him all the way because I was still getting used to his size, but I was getting better each time. At the rate I was going, next week, I would be deep throating his ten inches like it was nothing. Jacking his dick fast, I stayed on the end of his dick and sucked it like my life depended on it. I wanted to take his soul now so when we got to the house, he would be even more determined to take mine.

Knight stopped the car, and I assumed we were at a red light. His hand was on the back of my head, but he wasn't guiding me, just gripping my hair, which was turning me on even more. I sucked his dick sloppier, making it even wetter.

"Fuck! I'm about to nut."

Just as the words left his mouth, I felt his seeds shoot into my mouth and started flowing down my throat. I kept sucking and made sure to swallow every drop until his dick was empty. Satisfied, I sat back in my seat and opened the glove compartment to grab a napkin and wipe my hands that had spit all over them. Looking around, I saw that we were in the parking lot at a gas station and there were people here.

"Oh my God, Knight. What the fuck?" I looked at him with my eyes wide.

"Shit, what?" he looked confused.

"Why did you pull over in here? People probably saw us." I slapped his arm as he put his dick away and pulled his pants up.

"Man, nobody was paying attention. I have tinted windows, and if they did see, so what?" Knight shrugged his shoulders. "You with ya nigga. It ain't like you just out here sucking random dick."

"Next time, I'll just wait until we get to the house." I shook my head as I laughed, thinking about the situation. This nigga didn't even care.

"You want something out the store?"

"Just like a drug dealer, want to offer me something out the gas station. You got moneyyyyy," I joked, and he laughed.

"Grei, you fucking stupid. I'm just trying to offer ya ass something 'cause you just sucked the skin off my dick. Now, you want something or not?" he asked, dying laughing now.

"That is not funny." I rolled my eyes. "Yeah. I want some hot cheese popcorn, two of the small bags, with a hot sausage and a pickle. I don't care if it's in the bag or jar."

"You want just what the lil' ghetto chicks be eating. Let me find out you one of those."

"Whateverrr. Just hurry up, and don't talk to none of the ghetto chicks in the store."

"Nah, you the only ghetto bitch I want." Knight opened the door and got out the car. I watched as he walked to the door with so much swag. I loved watching the way he walked. It was confident, then it was dripping with thug and big dick. He walked into the store and was no longer in my eyesight.

Shaking my head at him, I pulled my phone out and pulled up Instagram. We had taken pictures before we came out, and we had so many likes and comments under it. It was hard trying to reply to everyone, and honestly, I was tipsy from all the drinks at the club. I liked everyone's comment and commented to a couple of people, then scrolled down my newsfeed.

There were a couple of people that posted pictures of them being in the club, but I hadn't seen them. It was so damn packed in there, and I was all in Knight's face, so shit, anybody could have been there. The door opened, and Knight got in the car.

"I got you a couple different flavors of pickles."

My eyebrows were raised as I looked over at him.

"What flavors? Pickles come in dill. That's it. That's all." I laughed.

"Look in there." Knight handed me the two bags that were filled with snacks. His ass had smoked a couple of blunts in the club and now had the munchies. There were chips, candy, and all types of shit. The first bag didn't have any pickles in it, so I opened the other bag. Knight put the car in gear and pulled out of the spot and out of the parking lot.

"Hot and spicy, zesty garlic." My face scrunched up as I read the names aloud. "I might try the hot and spicy one, but there's no way I'm eating the zesty garlic one." I put the pickles back in the bag.

"Ya head been getting better." Knight came from left field with the statement.

"What? What made you think of that? I was talking about pickles."

"Girl, I wasn't listening to you about them damn pickles. I'm thinking about that head you gave me that made me pull over to the gas station in the first place." Knight laughed and slapped his hand down on my bare thigh.

"Owww!" I yelled louder than I needed to as I pushed his arm in a playful manner.

"You better get used to that sting 'cause I'mma be slapping ya ass all night."

Whap!

He slapped my thigh again, this time not as hard. Just as I was about to talk shit, the light turned green, and Knight pulled off like he was in a race.

"What the hell? Why are you going so fast?" I look at him in the driver's seat, and he was looking in the rearview mirror. Looking back, I saw a black truck without their lights on, and they were on our ass.

"Turn around and sit back," Knight ordered me. "They been following us since the gas station." I didn't say anything as Knight swerved in and out of lanes and down side streets.

There weren't many people out tonight, but there were enough people out that we couldn't do a hundred on the street to get away from this truck. Every time I looked in the side mirror, they were right behind us, and we were nowhere even close to home. We wouldn't want them to follow us there anyway. Knight made a right turn down a side street then a quick left and turned our lights off.

The truck passed by the alley, and Knight started to slowly drive down the alley to the other end. Pulling out his phone, he put it on speaker.

"Yo?" I heard Cruz's voice come through the phone.

"Yo, I'm over here on Dewey, and some fucking truck following us. Where you at, nigga?"

"Shit, I'm still up here. I was getting some head from shorty, but I'm on my way. Shorty, you gotta chill. Move." We could hear shuffling around, and I couldn't do anything but shake my head. I guess everybody was getting head in the car tonight. "Send me ya locat—"

Boom!

As soon as we pulled out of the alley, the car was hit on Knight's side with so much force that Knight's head hit the steering wheel. I had my seat belt on, so my body was secured, but the right side of my head hit the window. The black truck was now on the left side of us and turned its lights on. I saw the doors open, and my heart started to beat out of my chest.

"Knight! Knight!" I shook Knight and tried to wake him up, but he was out cold. Unbuckling my seat belt, I searched the floor and Knight, trying to find the phone. My hands landed on a gun instead, and that was even better. Just as I went to grab the gun, the passenger door opened, and I was being pulled and lifted from the car.

"Get off me!" I started hitting, kicking, and punching, anything to get away. "Help! Help!" The street was quiet, but all I could hope is that someone heard me, or someone could help me.

I was carried to the truck and thrown into the back seat. The leather seats were cold against my skin, and the hairs on the back of my neck stood up as his hand touched my thigh. I knew it was him without him even saying anything. Looking up, there was Tommy, and I could tell he was high as a kite. His eyes were glossy, and he had sweat pouring down his forehead.

"Ahhh!" I screamed as he grabbed the back of my neck and squeezed.

"Didn't I tell you that you were mine forever?" Tommy spoke in my ear through gritted teeth.

Pow!

A gunshot rang out.

"Noooo," I cried out because I just knew that Knight had just gotten shot.

The front driver and passenger doors opened, and two men got in the car.

"Is he dead?" Tommy asked. His hand was still around my neck.

"Yeah, that nigga dead."

"Noooo, Knight. Noooo!" I cried out. At this point, I didn't give a fuck what happened to me. All I cared about was Knight being okay.

To Be Continued...

A NOTE FROM THE AUTHOR

Readers:
Thank you so much for reading part 1 of a new series. I hope you all enjoyed
it and will be back for part 2.

ABOUT THE AUTHOR

Residing in Rochester, NY, Misha grew up always having a love for reading. Reading urban fiction was her favorite pastime, and as she got older she realized what a talent she had in writing as well. Pursuing her dreams, Misha has penned a number of books and strives to get better with each work. Hopefully, you become a supporter and fall in love with each of her books one by one. Happy Reading!

STAY CONNECTED:

Like page: Author Misha
Readers group: Yamisha's Bookworm Boulevard

facebook.com/yamisha.williams
twitter.com/authormisha
instagram.com/_authormisha

ALSO BY MISHA

Jayceon & Rebecca: A Rochester Love Story (4 Book Series)

Sometimes I Trip On How Happy We Could Be (3 Book Series)

My Savage Loves Me Better (2 Book Series)

Loving You Until Your Last Breath (1 & 2 Short Stories)

Fallin' For A Boss's Love (3 Book Series)

Royalty Publishing House is now accepting manuscripts from aspiring or experienced urban romance authors!

WHAT MAY PLACE YOU ABOVE THE REST:

Heroes who are the ultimate book bae: strong-willed, maybe a little rough around the edges but willing to risk it all for the woman he loves.

Heroines who are the ultimate match: the girl next door type, not perfect - has her faults but is still a decent person. One who is willing to risk it all for the man she loves.

The rest is up to you! Just be creative, think out of the box, keep it sexy and intriguing!

If you'd like to join the Royal family, send us the first 15K words (60 pages) of your completed manuscript to submissions@royaltypublish-inghouse.com

LIKE OUR PAGE!

Be sure to <u>LIKE</u> our Royalty Publishing House page on Facebook!

CPSIA information can be obtained
at www.ICGtesting.com
Printed in the USA
LVHW04s1930180918
590557LV00017B/310/P